Dakota Dusk

Dakota Dusk

LAURAINE SNELLING

Published by eChristian, Inc.
Escondido, California

Mission Books

Dakota Dusk

Previously published as
Dakota Stories II: Dakota Dusk, Dakota December,
and Dakota Destiny by Smoky Water Press,
Post Office Box 2322, Bismarck, ND 58502-2322.
Smoky Water Press is a division of Capital Communications, Inc.
Bismarck, North Dakota. Former ISBN: 978-0-9820752-1-0

First printing in 2012 by eChristian, Inc.
eChristian, Inc.
2235 Enterprise Street, Suite 140
Escondido, CA 92029
http://echristian.com

ISBN: 978-1-61843-198-1

Published in association with the Books & Such Literary Agency, 52 Mission
Circle, Suite 122, PMB 170, Santa Rosa, CA 95409-5370, www.booksandsuch.com.

Scripture quotations are from the King James Version of the Bible.

Cover and interior design by Larry Taylor.

Produced with the assistance of Livingstone, the Publishing Services Division
of eChristian, Inc. Project staff includes Dan Balow, Afton Rorvik, Linda Taylor,
Tom Taylor, Jamilynne Taylor, Ashley Taylor, Lois Jackson, and Tom Shumaker.

Printed in the United States of America

19 18 17 16 15 14 13 12 8 7 6 5 4 3 2 1

Mission 🏛 Books

About the Author

L auraine Snelling is the best-selling author of over seventy books, both fiction and nonfiction, historical and contemporary for adults and young readers. Lauraine and her husband Wayne live in California with a Basset Hound named Winston.

To learn more about the author, you can visit www.laurainesnelling.com.

Read all the stories in this series:

Dakota Dawn

Dakota Dream

Dakota Dusk

Dakota December/Dakota Destiny

Dedication

To today's sons and daughters of the pioneers.

May we always remember those who came before us.

Chapter 1

"Ma, how would you like it if I moved back home?" Jude Weinlander dropped a kiss on his mother's cheek. "I know things ain't been goin' good for you. I . . . you . . . ah . . . the farm needs some work done, bad."

"You would do that?" Tall, iron-stiff Augusta turned from the black iron cookstove and waved a wooden spoon in the air. Shock and heat painted her face bright red.

"Well . . . uh . . . I'm kinda between jobs right now, so's Melissa, and I could stay around for a time, until you get someone to help you again, that is." Jude stuttered over the words while raking a hand through the dark blond curls that fell over his forehead in a charming tangle. He leaned his six-foot frame against the kitchen counter. The smile that had broken half of the female hearts west of the Mississippi and north of the Missouri erased the unaccustomed worry lines from his forehead and relit the flame in his clear, sky blue eyes.

Augusta left off stirring her pot of stew on the stove and sank into a chair at the square oak table, scarred and scuffed by years of hard use. She stared across the room at her son, a gleam of moisture evident in her faded blue eyes, eyes that had once matched those of the young man before her. "Have you spoken with Dag?" She pushed a strand of steel gray hair back into the bun at the base of her neck.

"Nah, why should I?" Jude pulled his rear away from the counter, snagged a chair out with his foot, and joined her at the table.

"He has been helping me out some with beans and flour and coffee and such," she said.

"Don't you keep the hens and cow no more?"

"Ja, sure, but the 'hoppers took the garden and I had no one to do the hay, so they got that, too." Augusta stared out the window. "Not been easy the last couple of years. My hired man quit this spring, you know. Sometime after you left town." She pushed herself to her feet as if the cares of the world were pounding her into the sod. "You want another cup of coffee?"

Jude nodded. "Things'll be easier now, Ma. You'll see." He accepted the chipped mug she offered him.

"Why?" Her tone sharpened. "You got some new scheme up your sleeve?"

"Not yet. Come on, Ma, I left off the cards and such. I aim to help you put this place back together. Dag ain't the only one in this family can take care of his ma." He patted her work-worn hand where it lay on the table. "You'll see."

"It'll be mighty fine having you home again." She sipped from her cup. "Where'd you leave Melissa?"

"She's at her ma's. Said I'd come first and make sure us coming here was all right."

"Son, this is your home. You're always welcome here."

"Not like some other places, huh?"

"You in some kind of trouble?" Augusta peered at him, as if delving behind the smile in his eyes to see if he was fooling her. When Jude employed this smile, the very angels would hand over their halos; its candlepower wasn't wasted on his mother. "Nah, Ma, come on. I just want to help you, that's all."

"I thank you, Son. I most surely do." Augusta straightened her shoulders. "Well, I'd best be gettin' at the chores. You want to milk old Betsy while I feed the hens? Then you can dig those spuds that made it through the 'hoppers."

"I . . . ah . . . I thought maybe I'd go for Melissa this morning. She don't take too well to staying with her ma. They don't get along much."

"Oh?" Augusta caught herself before her shoulders slumped, but barely.

"Don't get me wrong, Ma. I'll milk first." Jude held up a placating hand. He rose to his feet as if anxious to be at his work. "You still keep the bucket out in the well house?"

After the chores were finished, Jude hitched up the old horse to the ancient wagon and, leaving his saddle horse in the pasture, drove out of the yard. He watched the dust spurt up from beneath the horse's hooves and caught the caw of a crow, but otherwise the fall day stretched empty before him.

I've got to get some money, get some money. The thoughts kept time with the jangle of the harness and the *clumph, clumph* of the hooves in the dust. "Ya suppose there's a game going tonight in Soldahl?" he asked the world at large.

The crow circled overhead and cawed an answer.

"If only I didn't have to get Mellie. Sometimes women are more trouble than they're worth." He shook his head. *And this one ain't been worth much for some time.*

If only the baby had lived. Then he'd been one up on Dag. The first grandson, now that would have made his ma proud. But now that Dag was married, he'd probably have a whole houseful of kids.

Jude groaned and shook his hand at the persistent crow. Another trick on his brother gone sour. What a shock it had been to see the new Dag Weinlander—clean-shaven, neatly trimmed hair, decent clothes. Jude looked down at the new hole in the knee of his trousers. The cloth was so weak, it split when he knelt down to milk the cow this morning.

"It ain't fair. My brother, the dolt himself, has a thriving business, a beautiful wife, and that grand house of his. It just ain't fair, I tell ya." The old bay horse flicked its ears and kept up a nodding trot.

By the time Jude had driven onto the lane to his mother-in-law's farm, he had worked himself into a temper. The prosperous look of the farm did nothing to improve his mood. The look she gave him when she let him in the house could have curdled milk.

"Get your stuff. We gotta get back so's I can help Ma."

"I . . . I'm ready." Melissa dragged a scruffy carpetbag from another room. The effort made her catch her breath on a sob as she pushed a limp strand of dingy hair back from her face. "You hungry?"

"You got it ready?"

"No, but it'd just take a minute. I could slice you some bread and—"

"All right, just quit jawing and do it." Jude kept his gaze from wandering to his mother-in-law, but he could feel her glare stabbing him in the back.

Melissa scuttled over to the cupboard and, after slicing the bread and meat, put them together with butter. Then she poured coffee into a canning jar and, after a quick nod in her mother's direction, went to pick up her satchel. Bread and coffee in her hands, she looked from the carpetbag to her husband and back again.

Jude started for the door. At his mother-in-law's "Harumph," he snorted in disgust and whirled back to pick up the carpetbag. The glare he shot at Melissa made her sob again.

The trip home passed without a word. When Jude cast withering glances at Melissa, she studied her hands or the goldenrod nodding in the evening breeze along the side of the dusty road.

That night in bed, Melissa whimpered in her sleep. When she began to cough, Jude jerked the sheet over him and rolled over in bed. "Can't ya do something about that?" he snarled. "I need my sleep."

When Melissa returned to the bed, the smell of camphor floated around her like a mist. Jude sat up, glared at her in the moonlight, and, after punching his pillow, flopped on his other side. What he wouldn't do for a drink.

In the morning, Jude drove his mother and wife into town for church. After dropping them off, he aimed the horse toward the saloon at the other end of town.

He tied the animal to the hitching rack in front of the flat-fronted building and, after checking the locked door, walked around the back.

"Smitty, hey, Smitty. Open up," Jude called softly as he rapped on the door. The saloon wouldn't open until noon, but by then he should be back at the church to pick up the womenfolk.

"What now?" A rough voice called down from the flung-open window above.

"Hey, Smitty. How ya doin'?" Jude pushed the hat back on his head and grinned up at his friend.

"Well, well. If it ain't Jude come back to town. 'How ya doing' is right. Where you been?" The bartender leaned his elbows on the windowsill.

"Here and there. How about a bottle? I gotta get back and pick up the womenfolk after church or I'd stay for a game or two. How things been, anyhow?"

"Good, good. But not the same without you around. Sure you can't stay for a time or so?" A grin split the man's leathery face. He polished the top of his shiny pate with a cupped hand.

"Not this time, but I ain't gone for good. I'm helpin' my ma out some, you know how it is when they gets older. So I'll be around now and then." Jude shifted from one foot to the other. "What about that bottle or you gonna jaw all day?"

Smitty pulled his head back so fast he banged his head on the window.

Jude laughed and slapped his knee. "Better be more careful with my bottle. I got a thirst 'bout as wide as the Red in full flood." He grinned as he realized it was good to be back in Soldahl. Now, if he could just figure a way to get rid of the womenfolk. His fingers itched for the cards the way his throat did for that first swallow of good, solid whiskey.

The door of the saloon swung open in front of him. "Come on in then, you old buzzard." Smitty scratched himself and headed for the front of the saloon. "You heard about your brother?" He continued without waiting for an answer. "After he married that pretty little thing you brought over for him, they moved into the house with Mrs. Norgaard. In fact, as I heard it, the old lady deeded them two the house. Jude, you wouldn't recognize— you seen Dag yet?"

"Now, why would I want to see him? You think I been pining away for the sight of my brother or something?" Jude clapped his hat down on the counter and hung his rear over a bar stool.

"Nah. I just thought I should bring you up to date, so's you're not too surprised or something." Smitty slapped a bottle down on the bar. "That'll be four bits."

"Ah...I...uh...how about I pay for this later? I'm kinda short of cash right now."

Smitty paused for a moment. "You know, I—" He paused. "All right. Just this once. For old-time's sake."

Jude swung off the stool. "Thanks. If nothing else, I'll pay first hand I win." He raised a hand in farewell and headed out the door.

Once seated in the wagon, he broke the seal of the bottle and, lifting the bottle high, poured a generous slug down his gullet. He sighed and wiped his mouth with the back of his hand. It had been much too long between drinks.

He recapped the bottle and set it down in the back in between the burlap bags on the wagon bed. Now, after a stop at the mercantile for a store of tobacco, he'd head back for the church.

"Jude," the store owner said, slapping his hands on the counter before him and leaning across it. "If'n you ain't a sight for sore eyes. Gunna join us for a game tonight? I still gotta get that hunnert dollars back from the last round."

"Soon, soon. Anything new been happening whilst I been gone?"

"You seen Dag? Man, we sure done him a favor, bringing that pretty little gal over from Norway for him."

Jude felt a rage begin a slow burn down about his gut. If he heard about his wonderful brother one more time, he'd smash someone for sure. "Cut the jawing. You got any tobacco? And a couple of cigars. Better add some cheese, coffee, and some of those cinnamon twists. My ma always had a hankering for cinnamon twists." He stared around the well-stocked store as he waited for his order. Cracker and pickle barrels fronted the wooden counter. Boxes of the new dry cereal called cornflakes lined the shelves above the tins of spices. Rakes, hoes, and pitchforks hung from hooks above the boxes of boots and shoes. Kitchenwares filled one aisle and farm implements another.

One of these days, when his ship came in, Jude knew he would come in here and just buy whatever he needed. No more of this putting it on the slip and heming and hawing back and forth over what he could buy. Why, he needed new boots and—he stared down at the split leather on his ancient boots. All he really needed was one good night at the card table. One good night and he'd be back up on top again.

"Here ya go." Adam set the sack up on the counter. "Need anything else?"

"Not for now. Put that on my mother's tab for now. I'll settle up with you later."

"I don't know, Jude. Dag, he's mighty particular what goes on the bill, now that he's payin' it." He glanced up in time to catch the thundercloud racing across Jude's face. "But I'm sure this time'll be okay."

If I hear the name Dag one more time, I'll . . . I'll . . . Jude clamped a lid on his thoughts. He could put up with anything for a time. And what were the chances he'd be seeing his brother anyway? Dag surely didn't bring that highfalutin' wife of his out to the farm, and he sure didn't show up at the saloon to deal a hand or two.

He paused as he swung up into the wagon. Unless Dag had changed in those ways, too. Jude shook his head. Nah, no chance. He dug in the sack for the tobacco and, after stretching open the pouch, dug out a pinch and placed it between his lip and gum. Now that, that was mighty fine. A swallow of good whiskey and a chaw of tobacco. Now, if only he could add a card game to that, the day would be perfect.

He spat a brown gob of tobacco juice into the dirt as he drove the horse and wagon past the Norgaard house. So this is where his brother lived now. He's come up some since the soddie out on the plain. He spat again. Surely, there must be some way to bother his brother again. Some way that wouldn't backfire this time.

When he got to the church he ignored his mother's comments after handing her and Melissa up into the wagon. How could he get even? He jumped when he heard his mother mention Dag and Clara.

"They're what?" The question popped out before he had time to organize his thoughts.

"Dag and Clara are coming out to visit this afternoon. I told them I'd bake a cake, but she insisted they'd bring supper. Sure will be nice to have a treat again."

Jude dug down in the sack at his feet. "I got you a treat, something you always liked." He pulled out the cinnamon twists. "See, I think of you plenty."

"Why, thank you, you thoughtful boy," Augusta simpered in a totally uncharacteristic manner. She took a candy stick from the sack and passed the packet back to Melissa, who huddled on the wagon bed.

"No, thank you," she mumbled.

No, thank you, Jude mimicked in his mind. *Why can't I say no, thank you to Dag coming out? Why does he have to show up? All I heard about today was how great Dag is doing. Him and that wonderful wife of his.* Jude could feel the anger stirring again in his gut. The fire flickered and flamed as if doused by kerosene. He snapped the horse's reins and stamped his foot against the footrest.

All his life, Dag this and Dag that. And now his brother had a wife that all the town praised while his wife mewled from the back of the wagon. The flames flared higher.

The horse broke into a trot. Augusta clutched the side of the wooden bench. Jude heard a whimper from behind him. Even his mother had gone against him. Here she was, glad they were coming because they brought a good supper. He sucked the juice out of his chaw and spat it off the side of the wagon. It'd be a long time before he sat down to eat with his brother.

When they reached the farm, Jude leaped from the wagon, helped the womenfolk down, and trotted the horse down to the barn. He secreted his bottle down into the grain bin. Now he could take a swig when he needed one and no one would be the wiser.

As soon as the dog barked a welcome for Dag and Clara, Jude slipped out the back door, telling his mother he was off to do the chores.

"You be ready for supper in about an hour?" she asked as the door slammed behind Jude's hurrying form. He lurked behind the corner until he heard the visitors go inside the house.

The internal muttering continued while he threw grain to the chickens and walked out in the pasture to round up the milk cow. Usually she waited patiently beside the barn. But today everything was going wrong, even the cow. When he finally found her, laying down in a slight dip in the sparsely grassed field, chewing her cud, he hurried her up to the barn. Udder swinging, she trotted to the barn door and stopped. The look she shot him from over one shoulder would have rebuked a more tenderhearted man.

As Jude swung open the door, he slapped her on the rump. When he slammed the wooden stanchion bar in place, it pinched her neck. She lowed in protest.

Jude stomped off to the well house for the milk bucket. A slight smile lifted the corners of his mouth when he dug the grain out of the bin. His bottle lay snug in the bin, covered by the golden oats. His mouth watered at the thought. He brushed the grain away and lifted the bottle, sloshing the liquid inside. Did he dare? He shoved it back into its nest. Not now ... not with Dag on the prowl.

As he milked the cow, its milk streamed into the bucket, the *swish, swish* a music all its own. The milking song covered the sound of the door opening.

"Hello."

At the sound of his brother's voice, Jude jerked on the cow's teats. Before he could recover, the cow planted her foot squarely in the bucket and her tail whipped him across the eyes.

Jude leaped to his feet, milk running down his pant legs. "Did ya have to scare a body to death, creeping up thata way? Look what you made me do." He turned on his brother, fury transforming his handsome face to a mask of hatred.

"I'm sorry I startled you." Dag, his white shirt glistening in the dimness of the barn, crossed his arms over his chest. "But you and I need to talk and this is the only way I could see how to do so without the women around."

"I don't need to talk with you." Jude dumped the milk in a pan for the cats and, after rinsing the bucket out, returned to his stool. " 'Sides, I gotta finish here."

"I'll make this short and sweet. Ma says you have come home to help her out. We both know she needs help here since the last hired man quit. She can't manage all alone."

"I know. That's why I'm here." Jude returned to the squeeze and pull of milking.

"But the truth of the matter is that I've been bringing her supplies and paying her bills at the stores in town."

"So, you want a medal or somethin'?" Jude pushed his head harder against the cow's flank.

"No, I just don't want to see your tobacco on the tab. And I don't want to hear you're in town gambling and drinking. That would break Ma's heart, she's so glad to have you home again. So the rules are: no drinking, no gambling, and you buy your own tobacco and cigars."

"Who do you think you are, coming here and trying to tell me what to do with my life?" Jude stripped the last drops of milk from the cow's udder and shoved himself to his feet.

"I'm your brother, your older brother, and right now you need to join us for supper. Clara and Ma have it on the table. I'd like you to meet my wife since you had such a hand in bringing her to me. I never had a chance to thank you for that, you know." He offered his hand in gratitude.

Jude pushed aside the extended hand and, after releasing the cow, stalked off to the well house.

While the meal was indeed tasty, as Augusta had promised, Jude squirmed whenever he looked across the table to the woman who smiled so lovingly at his brother. Her laugh, her intense blue eyes, the golden hair waving down her back, the way she charmed his mother—they all irritated him. Especially when he glanced at the washed-out woman sitting beside him.

And the look of Dag himself. Had that man really been hiding under the dirt and stench of the blacksmith? And the way he talked. Why, one would think Dag had been to school for years. And Jude knew for sure that that hadn't been the case.

The apple pie Jude was eating was turning into prairie straw in his mouth. Jude shoved away from the table, mumbling that he had something he had to do. He didn't return to the house until everyone else had gone to bed.

The next few days did nothing to alleviate the anger festering in Jude's heart. A coyote raided the chicken house and killed three of their best laying hens. Every time Jude tried to fix something, he needed a new part or another piece of lumber or fencing wire. Only his secret friend buried in the grain bin consoled him.

One day the sun scorched the earth, ignoring the fact that fall was supposedly on the way. The sun burned down on Jude's head as he dug the few remaining potatoes and dumped them in the cellar. The cow came into estrus and broke through the fence to go visit the neighbor's bull, so he not only had to bring her back but had to repair the fence. All day his temper broiled along with the heat devils whirling away over the prairie.

Supper that day was a silent affair. Even Augusta relaxed her steel spine to sit down on the rear porch and fan herself with her apron.

"You'd think this was July rather than September," she said as she wiped the beads of moisture from her upper lip.

Jude merely grunted. The thought of his bottle down in the barn made his mouth prickle.

"Think I'll go on up to bed." Melissa stood in the doorway wiping her hands on her apron.

"Think I'll go on into town." Jude spit a gob of tobacco juice off the porch onto the hard-packed earth.

"What for?" Augusta jerked awake from her slight doze.

"Just to talk to the fellas at the mercantile. Find out where we can get some cheap grain. Not much left out in the barn."

"You won't go near the sa—" Melissa cut off her question at the fierce look Jude fired at her.

"You can go to the store tomorrow." Augusta drew herself up in the rocking chair. "It will be closed before you get there. The only place open in Soldahl at this hour is the saloon." Her voice brooked no argument.

"If I say I go now, I'll go—"

This time it was the mother's look that stopped the son.

Jude jerked open the screen door, shoved past his wife, knocking her against the counter, and stormed into the sitting room. He dug a cigar out of the humidor and stomped back into the kitchen to light it in the embers of the stove.

But instead of leaving by the back door, he returned to the sitting room.

After kicking the hassock into place in front of the brown velvet chair, he flung himself into the chair and propped his boots on the hassock. The puffs on his cigar sent spirals of smoke drifting to the high ceiling.

Who does she think she is to tell me what to do like that? His thought kept time with the billows of smoke. *A man should be able to do what he wants in his own house.* He shifted his dusty boots on the hassock, deliberately ignoring the tiny voice that reminded him of the household rules. No smoking in the house and no feet on the furniture. The only time the room was ever used was when company came.

Tonight Jude considered himself company. He ignored Melissa's quiet "Good night" and refused to respond when his mother started to say something. As the smoke cloud darkened around him, she snorted and made her way upstairs. A lesser woman might have marked her displeasure with heavy feet but not Augusta. Her feelings seemed to float back and freeze the room.

Jude called his mother every name he could think of and then created a few new ones, all in the regions of his mind, of course. When he finished with her, he started on Melissa. Why was he, of all men, so abused?

Sounds ceased from above except for the rhythmic snoring that indicated that his mother had fallen sound asleep. Jude listened carefully. Only the song of his bottle could be heard in the stillness of his mind.

Jude set his cigar on the edge of the small table beside the chair. If he hurried out, he could be back before anyone were the wiser.

The evening breeze that had felt so refreshing on the porch had increased to a wind, raising dust and dancing devils across the empty fields. The harvest moon shone down, lighting the path to the barn like midday.

Jude swung open the barn door and followed his nose to the grain bin. Practice made finding the bottle easy in spite of the darkness that encircled him like a comforting blanket. Out here, no one would try to tell him to remove his feet from the hassock. That's what footstools were for—resting feet. And chairs for bodies, especially tired bodies like his. His mind kept up the litany of complaints as he jerked the cork out with his teeth, dropped it in his hand, and raised the cool bottle to his lips. The first swallow was all he'd dreamed of.

Jude started to replace the cork, but a glance in the direction of the house and those interfering females made him take another.

After a couple more swigs, he edged his way over to the ladder to the haymow and, clutching his bottle to his chest, clamored up. He snuggled his backside down into the pile of hay and leaned back, exhaling a sigh at the silence and the comfort. No one would look for him here.

Soon his head fell back, the empty bottle slipped from relaxed fingers, and gentle puffings deepened into snores.

"What's—" Jude struggled up from the bowels of his sleep. What was the dog barking about at this time of night? He blinked, trying to decide where he was. After rubbing a hand across eyes filled with grit, he looked up to see gold lights dancing on the walls and ceiling above him. Was it morning already? He stumbled to his feet.

His mother would rip him limb from limb if she thought he spent the night drinking in the barn.

"Shut up, you stupid dog," he muttered as he fumbled for the ladder. "You'll wake the whole world if you haven't already."

When Jude stepped from the barn, his heart stopped in his chest. "Oh, no!"

Flames flickered within the downstairs windows of the house, smoke spiraling upward from the open windows.

Jude raced for the back door. His heart pounded in his chest. His mind pleaded for the God he so often profaned to help him get the women out. Surely the barking dog had awakened them, too.

"Ma! Melissa!" His screams rent the air. The wind tossed the sound away, creating instead its own monster song of roaring flames and crashing timbers.

Jude jerked open the door and, arm over his nose and mouth, stumbled through the smoke and heat, searching for the staircase.

Chapter 2

The heat beat Jude back. The dog leaped beside him, barking furiously at the flames. Jude choked and coughed, gagging for air as he leaned forward, nearly toppling to the ground. When he got his breath, he stumbled to the rain barrel at the corner of the house, soaked his shirt in the water, and wrapped the wet cloth around his face. After grabbing a deep breath, he charged through the back door.

The fire wasn't burning as furiously here as he made his way to the stairs. He couldn't call, saving every breath for the ordeal ahead. But the raging flames beat him out again. As his mind dimmed with the heat and smoke, he turned back. He never noticed the pieces of burning wood peppering his back or the heat searing his lungs. His final cry of "Ma" went no farther than his lips as he collapsed on the ground outside.

"Here he is!" the man yelled. "Jude's alive, I think."

"Ma, Melissa." Jude croaked.

"It's gone. All gone." The man draped a wet cloth over Jude's back and offered him a sip of water.

"Gone?" Jude tried to raise his head. Instead he collapsed into oblivion.

***

"Dag, I think he's coming around."

Jude heard the feminine voice from somewhere down in the chasm where he preferred to remain. At least down there, he didn't hurt so cruelly. His back, his head, his arms—all on fire. He twisted his face to the side. What was he lying on?

"Drink." He forced the word through lips that felt coated with some kind of grease. His throat spasmed around the single word.

"Here." A glass tube appeared between his lips and he sucked greedily.

Where am I? What's happened? The thoughts chased through his mind like the flames had—the flames—the house—Ma and Melissa. The memories seared his mind like the flames had seared his back. A groan tore from his heart and forced its way out his throat.

"Easy now." The voice belonged to his brother, Dag.

"Ma?"

"Send Mrs. Hanson for the doctor." Dag seemed to be talking from far away.

"Ma." Jude put all his energy into the request.

"Easy now, Jude. There's nothing more you can do. You're at my house and burned terribly. It's a miracle you're still alive."

Jude digested the words. But what about his mother and Melissa? Had they gotten out? He could hear the roar of the flames, the dog barking. Were there screams? He tried to remember.

"How about another drink?" The tube appeared again.

Jude drank gratefully. The cool water slipped down like the elixir of life itself. He fought the pain and the fog trying to blanket his mind. "Ma!"

"She's gone, Jude. Both of them."

The simple words sent him spinning back into oblivion. Pain and searing agony brought him back.

The tube appeared and, as before, he drank, sucking in the life-giving moisture. He tried to figure out what he was lying on, but the effort was too great. Instead, he let himself slip back to that no-man's-land. The pursuing flames of his nightmares hurt far less than the thought of Ma and Melissa dying in the fire.

"How do you think it started?"

Jude heard the voice and fought against the pull back to reality. How did he think it started? How would he know? He'd been out in the barn, slugging down his nightly antidote for living.

"Maybe a lamp?" This voice rang with feminine sweetness.

"We may never know. It was an accident pure and simple." The gruff voice belonged to a stranger. Who was it?

"Thank you for coming, Doctor."

Ah, that's who it was. He'd heard the voice before, sometime during the long, long night.

"You take care of yourself now, too, you hear?" Footsteps faded along with the voice.

While Jude kept his eyes closed, he couldn't shut off his mind. Ma was always so careful. She always banked the stove. Only used candles in an emergency. How did the fire start? Had there been a lightning storm? He tried to shrug his shoulders to relieve the itching. Instead, he bit his lip against the fiery pain.

"Drink." He swallowed and forced his voice to obey the command to speak louder. "Drink, please." The tube appeared at his lips again and he sucked greedily.

"Jude, we have to get some nourishment into you so I'm going to give you some broth by the tube now. Can you manage that?"

Jude knew Clara's voice by now. He nodded.

This time the drink was warm and tasted of beef and onion.

"How long since the fire?" Jude raised his head and turned to the side so he could see. This laying on his stomach was getting hard to handle.

"A week." Dag sat down on the floor in front of his brother so they could look each other in the face. "How are you feeling?"

"Guess I'll live."

"We were afraid you were gone, too, there for a time." Dag crossed his legs and leaned against the wall. "Dr. Harmon says it's a miracle you made it."

"He the one who rigged this bed?"

"No, I did." Dag ducked his head in the old habit of humility. "When he said you couldn't be on your back and you looked like you'd smother on your stomach, I built this. Clara padded it with quilts."

"I allus knew you could make whatever was needed." Jude's voice took on a dreamy quality. It was like looking through a telescope backwards. "Pa said you was one clever boy, even when you was a kid."

"What?"

"That's why I teased you so much."

"Jude, you're talking through your head. Or are you delirious again?" Dag shook his head with a snort.

"Nah. I hated you sometimes . . . most of the time, you know."

Jude let his mind float down the telescope. The pain met him halfway down. He slipped off without answering Dag's last question. How would he know how the fire started?

Just before the blackness claimed him completely, he saw the cigar, smoking on the table in his mother's sitting room. His cigar! The one he'd left when he headed for the barn. The pain now searing his heart made the pain from his back seem like a hangnail.

When Jude awoke he wished he were dead. Why didn't they let him die? He wasn't worth keeping alive. He clenched his teeth and arched his back. The pain drenched him and nothing could erase the agony in his mind. His carelessness killed both Ma and Melissa. How could he live? Why bother?

"Jude, what is it? The pain is worse?" Clara knelt in front of him. "Can I get you something?"

Jude shook his head. He couldn't tell her. How could he tell anyone?

"Here. I made you some chicken broth this time. Doc says you can have whatever you can swallow. But I know that position makes eating difficult."

Her caring words drove the nail deeper. He didn't deserve anyone taking care of him like this. He clenched his teeth against the tube she held to his mouth. *God, please let me die.* He felt like roaring at whatever it was had kept him alive and let them die.

"Jude, you have to eat." Dag took his place against the wall. "It's been two days now and you haven't taken even a sip of water. What is it?"

Jude left the land of the screaming voices and raised his head to look at his brother. Couldn't he tell? Wasn't it written across his forehead—MURDERER—in giant red letters.

Jude took a wet cloth and wiped his brother's face. "Doc says you can get up tomorrow if you are strong enough. He says if we don't get you moving, you'll lose all the muscle tone in your back."

Jude clenched his teeth. All right, tomorrow he'd get up. The sooner he got better, the sooner he could leave. Since he wasn't dying this way, he could take care of the matter better when he could ride away. He took the offered drink and grunted his thanks.

From then on Jude gritted his teeth against the pain and forced himself to down all the fluids and nourishment he could stand. He did exactly as the doctor ordered, all except the laudanum. He refused to let his mind dwell in that no-man's-land that the drug brought with it. He didn't deserve the release.

He still couldn't lie on his back, so he slept on the slotted bed Dag had devised, where his head fit into a brace and looked straight down. In that position, Jude found he didn't have to look at anyone unless he wanted to. And he didn't so choose.

One afternoon when he was lying there, he heard Clara, the doctor, and Dag speaking in the other room while they thought he was sleeping.

"But he was doing so much better. I can't understand the change," Clara said.

"Ja, it's not like Jude to be so silent." Dag's voice sounded weary.

"He's been through a lot. Sometimes accidents like this completely change a person." Doc paused before continuing. "Thought for a while there when he quit eating and drinking we was gonna lose him after all."

Ah, if only it were that easy, Jude thought. *After all the meanness I've bothered my brother with all these years, I couldn't quit and die on him in his own home. How can the man treat me with such love and gentleness when all these years . . .* His mind drifted back, picking out the instances of his cruelty and he winced.

If his mother's ideas of the Maker's judgments were true, he'd not be standing in line for angel's wings, that's for sure. He had to get well enough to get out of here soon. The thought of being a continued burden ate at him like a canker. He studied the healing burns on the back of his hand and arm; his back they said was worse. The angry red welts glistened under the healing salve Mrs. Hanson kept forcing him to apply. At least now when she spread it on his back, he could stand the touch. Soon, he would be able to wear a shirt and then he could leave.

The thoughts of the bustling housekeeper seemed to bring her to him.

"Time for more cold cloths and medicine," Mrs. Hanson said.

Her cheery voice could change in an instant if he didn't respond. He'd learned that the hard way. He knew he was only here on sufferance. While she tolerated him, he could tell from her eyes she wouldn't hesitate to toss him out.

He turned his head when he heard a cane tapping along with a much lighter step and entering his room. Mrs. Norgaard leaned on her cane, but he couldn't raise his head far enough to see her face.

"If we move that chair over by the wall," Mrs. Norgaard said, "I shall be able to converse with our patient more easily." Mrs. Hanson huffed but did her employer's bidding, and Mrs. Norgaard settled herself into her chair in her normal pose, back ramrod straight and never touching the back of the chair.

Silence descended on the room as she studied the man on his stomach. Jude studied the spot on the floor immediately below his face.

Why doesn't she say something? Why don't I say something? The thoughts tiptoed around his mind, fearful the woman in the chair could read them. Jude cleared his throat. Why was she here? Had she come to see him before, when he was unconscious? Had he said anything to her he shouldn't have?

He could feel her eyes drilling into the top of his head. The regrowing hair tingled in response. This was as bad as being called before the class back when he was in school.

Did she suspect the fire had been his fault? That a cigar, the one he'd been warned to not smoke in the house, burned his wife and mother to death. He felt the twisting between his mind, heart, and gut. If she knew, surely she would have thrown him out long ago.

He could stand it no longer. He raised his head, refusing to flinch when the wrinkling skin of his neck and upper back sent pain rippling and stabbing. It wasn't judgment he saw in her eyes. No, they were the eyes of love. Compassion flowed from her to him as if they were bound by golden cords.

He could feel tears burn at the back of his eyes. Tears! *Grown men don't cry.* The order failed to stem the flow. Jude sniffed as quietly and subtly as possible. He blinked not only once but several times, but still one fat tear managed to escape and drip off the end of his nose.

Why didn't she say something? Who turned on the furnace? The room seemed to have heated up twenty degrees or so.

Still, the silence stretched . . . and stretched. But Jude was the one who felt like he was being pulled apart, limb from limb.

"I want to thank—" he cleared his throat and started again. "Thank you for . . . aah . . . having me here . . . in your house."

"This is no longer my home. It now belongs to Dag and Clara."

"Oh." Then the rumors were true.

"They've become my family."

Silence settled in again. Why in the world did he feel like crying?

Jude gritted his teeth. When that didn't help, he bit his bottom lip. Even the taste of blood failed. One didn't yell at a lady. His mother had drilled that into him from the time he was little, but that didn't prevent him from screaming in his head. His body, the fire, the tears, the pain, the heat, the—he ran out of things to scream about.

"It will do no good." The words crept past the damaging words and shut him right down.

"Huh?" He threw his head up as far as possible. "Oh—" He stopped abruptly, but the grimace said more than he intended.

"All the anger you harbor. It will only cause you more pain."

Jude shook his head. If she only knew. The silence seeped in again.

How could she sit so still? He felt his fingers twitch . . . then his toes. He felt like twitching all over. Itching . . . twitching . . . Oh, how he could use a drink!

"When you can accept our forgiveness, it will always be here. Dag and Clara can live no other way and neither can I. Always remember that." She rose to her feet and walked to the door. "Remember, too, that Christ died so we might live forgiven. We all might live so. Good evening, Jude." Her footsteps echoed faintly down the hall.

In the morning he was gone.

Chapter 3

G et outa here before I ... I ..."
    "Before you what?" The voice held a trace of a leer that she was sure matched the face hidden in the dimness. "There's no one to hear you. Ma and Pa are gone for the night, remember?"

Rebekka Stenesrude swallowed to dislodge the fear clogging her throat. She could feel the perspiration running down her back under the flannel nightgown. Why hadn't she gone to stay in town when she learned that Mr. and Mrs. Strand were going to be gone? She listened carefully, waiting for the man—if you could call him that—to move again so she could determine where he was standing. Why, oh why, had she drawn the heavy draperies? If only the moonlight were lighting the room. But then he could see her more clearly, too.

A devilish chuckle echoed from the darkened corner. The sound caused the hairs on the back of her neck to stand at attention. Why hadn't she been more alert? She'd noticed his smiles and secret glances, but fighting off advances of young men had never been a problem as there'd never been any to fight off or even brush away.

Her antennae strained to sense the attacking man. What could she do? She felt carefully behind herself, seeking something with which to strike her attacker. Her fingers closed over the handle of the heavy pitcher on the commode.

"You can't run fast enough to get away and if you scream, well, who's gonna hear you?"

The voice sent shivers rippling up her back again, but at least now she knew which way the attack would come from. She took a deep breath in an attempt to slow her thundering heart and then flexed her fingers so she could grip the handle more firmly.

Suddenly, he came with a rush, shoving her against the commode. She swung with all her might. The pitcher crashed against him. Both the man and the shards struck the bare floor at the same time.

The scream died in her throat. She leaped for the door, expecting him to follow, but only silence and her tortured breathing filled the room. Was he dead?

Rebekka grabbed her clothes off the hooks on the wall and ran down the stairs. When she paused to listen, she heard a groan. Relieved in one way but furious that she hadn't permanently silenced the oaf, she darted out the door. "Please, God, let a horse be in the barn." The muttered prayer matched the rhythm of her pounding feet.

In the darkness of the barn, she ripped a bridle off the wall and, with outstretched hands to guide her, made her way to the horse stalls. "Thank You, Lord." She took in a deep breath so she wouldn't panic the horse in the stall. Murmuring gentle words, she shuffled carefully to the animal's head and slipped the bridle on over the halter. Each action seemed to take an hour as she fumbled in the darkness. After untying the slipknot, she backed the animal out of the stall. Then, after retrieving her clothes from where she'd laid them on a bar by the door of the stall, she led the animal outside.

A roar of pain and anger could be heard clear from the house to the barn as Rebekka led the horse over to the edge of the watering trough, stepped up, and swung herself astride the horse, her nightgown and housecoat bunched up around her knees.

Adolph Strand crashed the screen door against the wall and staggered out on the porch, clutching his head.

Rebekka dug her heels into the horse's ribs and galloped down the lane. Where would she go in the middle of the night? Thank God Mr. and Mrs. Strand were driving the team and there was no way Adolph could follow her.

A mile or so from the farm, she pulled her horse down to a jog. A full moon directly overhead bathed the land in silver and each leaf and blade of grass shimmered with the heavy dew. A sleepy bird called from somewhere, perhaps the brilliant light of the moon confusing his inner clock. Rebekka drew in a deep breath, the aroma of a steaming horse mingling with some night-blooming flower.

"What a shame not to enjoy a night so marvelous as this." She tipped her head back, luxuriating in the feeling, but shivered again at the thought of what had nearly happened to her. Stirred by the breeze and the night scents, she inhaled again. If only she could keep riding forever.

Rebekka shook her head and made an unladylike snort, matching that of the horse she rode. Forever would be a long time, and she had school in the morning. No matter what had happened tonight, all twenty-one of her students would greet her in the morning with bright and shiny faces. And the schoolmarm must be above reproach. Not riding around the country in the moonlight—in her nightgown and housecoat.

She shuddered again at the thought of how close she'd come to losing that purity required of schoolmarms. That . . . that, she couldn't think of a name vile enough. But to whom could she talk? Who would believe her? She clamped her lips together.

Willowford had been her home now for two years and surely, in that time, the parents of her students must trust her. They must—she shook her head. But they could never be told. The Strand family had lived in the area for twenty years or more, and it would be her word against theirs.

She lifted her face to the moon, staring beyond the silver disk to the star-studded midnight expanse of the heavens. "Father God, what do I do? Where can I go? Your word says You look out for widows and orphans. How about an old-maid schoolmarm?"

She waited, her body relaxed and swaying with the moving horse. Would the stars sing for her, bringing the message she needed? She pulled the horse to a halt to listen better. *Moses had his burning bush,* she thought. *How will God talk with me?*

A bird twittered in the brush in the ditch. A breeze lifted the horse's mane and billowed her nightgown and housecoat. She smoothed them down and dropped her chin to her chest. How silly she was being. God didn't talk to people on earth anymore. Did He?

She nudged the horse into a slow jog; its tapping hooves drowned out the night music. A picture of the Widow Sampson's boxy white boardinghouse came into her mind. Maybe she could at least stay there until she spoke with Mr. Larson, the school superintendent for the district.

"One thing sure," she promised the trotting horse, "I won't go back to the Strands', no matter what anyone says. I'll be on that train for . . . for anywhere first." The horse's ears flicked back and forth, and he snorted as if in perfect agreement.

When they entered the darkened town, she slowed the animal to a walk. Music echoed from the saloon and bright light formed a square clear out to the middle of the street. Rebekka edged the horse to the other side of the packed-dirt street and nudged him back into a trot. She couldn't be seen in dishabille like this and still live and teach in Willowford.

After following the picket fence around to the back of the widow's boardinghouse, Rebekka slid off the horse and onto the ground. She tied her mount to the rail and opened the gate. Rebekka froze as the screech of the hinges echoed loud enough to wake the sleepers halfway down the block.

Then, a dog barked on the other side of the street and her horse rubbed his chin on the picket, sending his bit a-jingling.

Rebekka tiptoed up the walk, her hand at her throat. She paused again when the first step squeaked beneath her bare foot. How could she rouse the Widow Sampson without waking all her boarders?

She tapped lightly on the back door. When nothing happened, she tapped again more firmly. "Please, please," she whispered to the heavens. But, instead of a welcome from within, she heard someone making his way down the street, singing, if one could call it that, a barroom ditty.

Rebekka formed a fist and raised her hand. She paused just before banging as a disgruntled voice came from within the house.

"Just hold on to your britches. I'll be there soon's I can." Other grumbles followed, along with the slap of carpet slippers on a wooden floor. "Who's there?" The words were matched by the door's opening just enough for a mobcapped woman to peek around the door.

"Widow Sampson."

"Why, if'n it ain't the schoolmarm. Miss Stenesrude, what are you doing here this time of night—and in your nightclothes? You're not needing a nurse, are you?" When Rebekka shook her head, the door opened all the way. "Get yourself in here before you catch your death."

"Thank you, I . . . I can explain." Rebekka looked over her shoulder to where her horse tossed his head and tried to reach the tips of the grass growing along the fence. She clutched her spare clothes to her body and then handed them to the older woman. "But first I better see to the horse. Do you have a place I can put him for the night?"

Widow Sampson accepted the clothing and pursed her lips. "Why, I s'pose you can put him in the shed there. We're a mite low on coal right now, so there should be room. He your horse?"

"No. I'll explain as soon as I return." Rebekka started down the steps and turned back. "Have you a rope or something I can tie him with?"

"Uh, just a minute." The older woman shut the door.

A shiver attacked Rebekka now that the danger was nearly past. She could hear the singing coming nearer. Did the man have to come down this street? What if he lived in the next house? Rebekka wrapped her arms around her shoulders to quell more of the bone-rattling quakes.

The door reopened and Widow Sampson stepped out on the porch. "Here you go. Think you can see well enough or should I bring a lantern?"

They both paused in response to the off-key serenade. "Oh, that man! He would choose tonight to drink himself silly. How Emma puts up with that, why, I'll never know. You get into the shed and keep that horse quiet until Elmer goes on by. Of course he wouldn't remember if he saw you or not, but best not to take any more chances." She handed Rebekka the coiled rope as she talked and shooed her toward the waiting animal.

Rebekka gladly did as Mrs. Sampson said, keeping her hand over the horse's nostrils when it was inclined to nicker at the man weaving his way past them. As soon as the fellow turned into his own gate and stumbled up the stairs to his house and through the door, she stripped off the bridle and knotted the rope, both into the halter and around a post. "I'll feed you in the morning," she whispered. After a quick hug and pat in total gratitude, she hurried back to the house.

In the meantime, Widow Sampson had lit a lamp and seated herself at the oilcloth-covered table, where she'd set a plate of sugar cookies and two glasses of buttermilk. "Here, I thought some refreshment might be in order since I think your tale may take more than a moment or two." She gestured to the chair,

Rebekka sank into it gratefully. Another shiver shook her frame as she wrapped her feet and legs around each other for warmth. "Thank you for letting me in." She clamped her teeth against a shiver.

"My, my, child, you've gone and caught your death." The widow pushed herself to her feet. "I'll be right back. You need something to warm you right now." Her carpet slippers slip-slapped into a bedroom just behind the kitchen.

Rebekka waited. She could hear the squeak of a chest lid raising and Mrs. Sampson digging around for something. In a minute the woman returned, her cheeks bright red from the effort and her white lawn mobcap set slightly off to the right, giving her the look of a merry elf. "Here ya be," she said as she draped a blanket around Rebekka's shoulders and handed her a pair of hand-knit woolen socks. "These oughta warm you up."

Rebekka leaned forward to slip the socks over her freezing toes. She wasn't sure if her last shudder was from the cold that seemed to penetrate her clear to the bone or if it was the residual fear with the same knifing intensity. How close she'd come to the brink of losing her life the way she knew it. "Thank You, Lord, thank You." Her words kept pace with the carved clock standing sentinel at the door to the dining room.

She drained the last of the buttermilk and set the glass down carefully so as not to disturb the silence. When she looked up, Mrs. Sampson smiled and reached over to pat the younger woman's hand.

"Ja, you are safe here, now. You know you can tell me what happened and it will go no farther than these very walls."

Rebekka nodded. Did she want to tell? She could feel the flush of embarrassment flaming in her cheeks. What words could she use? What really had happened? She chewed on the inside of her right cheek and clutched the blanket closer around her.

"Our Lord says confession is good for the soul and that don't mean only what we done wrong. Now, I know for certain you wouldn't be here in the middle of the night in your nightclothes if something powerful terrible hadn't happened." She studied the face of the young woman before her. "And I know, too, you weren't to be at fault. Not intentionally anyhows."

Rebekka struggled to talk past the chunk of prairie dirt clogging her throat. Dirt, that's what it was all right. What he was. She swallowed again. "I . . ."

"Take your time, dear, we're in no hurry."

"I'd gone to bed. This is my month out at the Strands', you know, and Mr. and Mrs. are gone to her sister's for a few days." Tears burned at the back of her eyes and down her throat. She squeezed her eyes against the burning and rolled her lips together.

At the feel of the other woman's hand on her own, the tears and fears burst forth and Rebekka laid her head on her arms, the sobs shaking her shoulders. "He . . . he came at me." Great gulping sobs punctuated her words. She wiped her face on the blanket and tried to sniff the flow back again, but failed miserably.

Mrs. Sampson let her guest cry. She patted the younger woman's arm, "there, there nows" a descant to the guttural sobs. As an occasional sniff replaced the storm, the widow pushed herself to her feet and crossed to the stove to dip a cloth in the warm water of the reservoir on the back of the iron-and-chrome behemoth.

"Here." She handed the cloth to Rebekka. "Now wash your face and hands while I get you a glass of water. Then we'll talk, if you feel up to it."

Rebekka nodded and did as told. How wonderful it felt to be taken care of, like her mother had done back in the good years before—she slammed the door in her mind that had opened just a crack. Stay with the here and now; no good looking back.

The chair creaked as Widow Sampson sat back down. She had set two glasses of water on the table. "I could start up the stove and make coffee," she said as she pushed one glass over to Rebekka, "but the noise might wake up my boarders and that wouldn't be very kind."

"I . . . I never thought, I mean—I thought you'd have room for another. Are your rooms full, then?" Rebekka's heart took up that erratic thumping again. What would she do if . . . ?

"Now, now, just don't you worry yourself none. I got a room for you. Why, Mr. Prescott moved out just two days ago. I cleaned it all right nice again, so you can see, it's just waiting for you. Nice corner room it is, too."

Rebekka inhaled a sigh of pure relief At least something was going right. She wiggled her feet in the wool socks, scooting them back and forth on the floor and then wrapping them together under the chair. She brushed an errant tear from the corner of her eye. Why had this happened to her?

"Well, as I started to say," and the words drifted off as her mind returned to the farmhouse. She clamped her jaw against the fury she could feel exploding in her chest. "He attacked me! That . . . that—" She couldn't think of any words bad enough. "And he thought I was funny. He was laughing. Until he rushed me and I hit him."

"You hit him?"

"With the pitcher from the commode. When he crashed to the floor, I grabbed my clothes and ran out the door." She continued with her story, not leaving out any details.

"Well, I never."

"I never either. And now I don't know what to do. Can I please stay here until I talk with Mr. Larson, the superintendent? I . . . I can pay." She could feel her mouth drop open. "At least, I can if I can get my things from their house. But I have money in the bank, too . . . some." She raised her gaze from studying her clenched fists.

"Now, don't you worry. Why, when we tell Lars what happened, he'll go out there personally and whip that young pup. Surely the sheriff could do something about this."

"No!"

"No?"

"Don't you see, I can't tell anyone. If this story gets around, I'll lose my position. Teachers are fired for a lot less reason than this."

"But it wasn't your fault." The words exploded from the widow's lips. She caught herself. "I know. I know. The snickers. The men will all get together and say you enticed him. That's what Adolph'll tell anyone who asks."

"I know. And those who don't. What can I do?"

"Let me think on this, child. You go on and get a good night's sleep and we'll let the good Lord tell us what to do. He never makes mistakes." The older woman sighed and shook her head.

"You . . . you believe me, don't you?" Rebekka pushed her cuticle back with a trembling finger. She looked up to see Mrs. Sampson smiling at her.

"Yes. Have no doubts in your mind about me. And God, who knows your heart, will work this out. God has a plan in mind, you can be sure of that."

"I know . . . I think." Rebekka caught herself on a yawn. She pushed herself to her feet. "And you . . . you won't tell anyone? Not ever?"

"Come along, my dear. That question don't even bear an answer." Mrs. Sampson picked up the kerosene lamp and led the way up the stairs. She opened the second door on the right. "The bed's all made up. I'll bring up warm water in the morning, but usually my guests come downstairs for their own. Breakfast will be at seven, prompt. Mrs. Knutson has to open her shop at eight." She set the lamp down on the five-drawer oak dresser and dug a spill from the drawer to light the room's lamp from the one she brought in.

Rebekka stared around in delight as the warm glow of the kerosene lamp brought to life the rainbow colors in the log cabin patchwork quilt on the spindle bed. A hand-crocheted doily kept the matching pitcher and bowl from scratching the top of the commode; a braided rag rug lay by the bed, ready to keep feet off the cold floor on a winter morning.

"Oh, this is beautiful." She looked around to find brass hooks on the back of the door and hung up her dress.

"I have an armoire in the storage room that I could bring in here for you to hang up your clothes. If you decide to stay, that is."

She chuckled at the sight of the younger woman trying to disguise another yawn. "You go on to sleep now. Nothing can hurt you here." She picked up her lamp and closed the door behind her with a quiet click.

Rebekka felt the bottom of her night dress and realized it was damp. But, she had nothing else in which to sleep. She'd just pulled back the covers when she heard a tap on the door. "Yes?"

Mrs. Sampson peaked through the crack in the door and held out a faded flannel nightgown. "Here, yours is still damp, I'm sure. Don't want to take a chance on you coming down with something."

"Thank you." Rebekka crossed the room and accepted the offering. "You are so kind."

"Ja, well you need some kindness right now." She harrumphed her way back out the door.

"Oh, Lord above, what am I going to do?" Rebekka either prayed or pleaded, she wasn't sure which, after she snuggled down under the crisp sheets. If she told Mr. Larson exactly what had happened, would he believe her or throw her out? If she didn't tell him, how would she explain the need to leave the Strand farm before the school year was up? Where would she go? She allowed her gaze to drift around the peaceful room, where the moon cast bright spots upon the waxed floor and the sheer curtains fluttered in the night breeze. She gulped back a leftover sob. Resolutely, she climbed from the bed and knelt on the rug.

"Heavenly Father, I have to leave this in Your hands. I don't know what to do. I thank You for sending Your angels to protect me." She shuddered again at the memory. "Please, if it be Your will, I would be pleased to stay in Willowford. Thank You again. Amen." She rose to her feet and slipped back into the cooling bed. The idea of closing her eyes and letting the memories surge back was about as frightening as the actual event.

She rubbed her cold feet together and then snuggled them up into the folds of the nightgown. Warmth stole around her, rich and comforting, like the sense of peace that crept along into her heart. On a gentle sigh, her eyelids drifted closed. When they fluttered open one last time, she smiled at the thought. There were two smiling angels sitting at the foot of her bed. What a wondrous dream.

She greeted the morning cockcrow with a catlike stretch, starting with her arms and working down clear to her toes. "Thank You, Father," she breathed at the thought of the restful sleep she'd had—no nightmares... no memories. She sat straight up. But what about the angels? She chuckled as she left the bed and went to stand in front of the window.

Dawn had bowed out, giving way to sunrise and the glorious birdsongs greeting the new day. The aromas of freshly turned earth and the green shoots sprouting up to meet the sun drifted in on a teasing breeze.

A tap at the door caught her attention. "Just your warm water, dear." The cheery voice brought a smile to Rebekka's face.

"Come in, Mrs. Sampson." Rebekka hurried across the floor to open the door. "Thank you so much." She stepped back to let the bustling housekeeper in.

"And how did you sleep? Was the bed all right?" She set the pitcher in the bowl on the oak stand and placed the towel draped over her arm beside the bowl. "There's soap there. I made it myself. I add rose petals for the fragrance." She peered into her guest's face. "You look rested, in spite of all you went through." She patted Rebekka's arm. "Breakfast in half an hour." And out the door she went.

Rebekka clapped her mouth closed, sure now that she understood how one felt after being whirled around in one of the summer tornadoes. Then she took her white blouse and dark skirt down from their hook and shook them to dislodge both horsehair and wrinkles. After laying them across the bed, she poured water into the bowl. As she picked up the soap, she inhaled its faint fragrance. What a luxury after the lye soap she'd been forced to use on the Strand farm.

After washing, Rebekka stared from her nightgown to her skirt and blouse, then to her feet. She had no underthings and no shoes. How could she call on Mr. Larson like this?

She combed her fingers through her hair and wished for the brush and comb sitting on her dresser at the farm. All of her things. She had to retrieve them, but how?

Teeth clenched against the surging anger, she pulled the nightgown back over her head and picked up the white blouse. Noticing smudges on the front and sleeves, she took the garment over to the washstand and applied the soap and water and some hard scrubbing to remove the stains. She dried the blouse as much as possible and smoothed the damp surface with her fingers. All the while doing this, she brooded over the injustice of it all.

It wasn't her fault! But if it wasn't, why did she feel so guilty? Why did she feel like she should wash again and keep on scrubbing?

She shoved her arms into the sleeves and buttoned the pearl buttons, then put on her walnut brown serge skirt. Standing in front of the mirror, she finger-combed her hair again and braided it, clamping the end with her fingertips until she could ask Mrs. Sampson for some pins.

As she made her way down the stairs, she could hear two women's voices coming from the kitchen. A canary trilled when they laughed, adding his music to the homey scene. Rebekka paused in the doorway.

The round table was now set for three, a pot with bobbing pink cabbage roses set between the cut-glass salt and pepper shakers and a gleaming golden mold of butter.

The gold-and-black canary hopped about his cage in the front of the window, pipping his song as if he were responsible for the coming of the new day.

Rebekka cleared her throat. "All, good morning."

"Oh, there you are." Widow Sampson turned from stirring her kettle on the gleaming black stove. "Mrs. Knutson, you know Rebekka Stenesrude, the schoolmarm, don't you?"

A diminutive woman, as slim as Widow Sampson was round, nodded and smiled at the same time. "Of course. I . . . ah—" She ducked her chin and made as if to sit down then paused from fussing with the chair. "If there's anything you need . . ."

Rebekka tore her gaze from the other boarder to stare helplessly at Mrs. Sampson. When the older woman barely shook her head, Rebekka breathed again. Thankfully, she hadn't told the secret.

"I mean, Alma said you had to leave your things. Whatever I have that you can use, you are welcome to it." Her voice faded into a whisper. "I don't want to be presumptuous . . . or anything."

Rebekka felt like circling the table and wrapping the bitty bird of a woman in her arms. Instead, she clamped her fingers over the back of the chair in front of her. "Thank you." She picked up the end of her braid. "You wouldn't by any chance have extra hairpins, would you?"

"Oh, yes." A bright smile lighting her face, the little woman darted out the door and up the stairs.

"Never worry, your secret is safe with me, but I had to tell her something." Mrs. Sampson placed a filled bowl of oatmeal at each place. "I have a plan. We'll talk when she leaves for her shop."

Abigail Knutson returned and placed pins and a comb and brush by Rebekka's place. "There, and now, let's eat. I mustn't be late."

After grace, the three women chatted happily while eating their biscuits and jam besides the oatmeal and coffee. Rebekka wiped her mouth with the napkin she'd spread on her lap and tucked it back into the carved wooden napkin ring. "Thank you. I haven't enjoyed breakfast like this in a long time." She raised a hand and shook her head when Mrs. Sampson tried to refill the coffee cup.

Mrs. Knutson left immediately after placing her breakfast things in the sink. "Now you remember, if I can help with anything, you be sure to tell me."

Rebekka nodded and rose to take her things to the sink, also.

"Now." Mrs. Sampson sat back down after the front door closed. She lifted her coffee cup to her mouth and, after a sip, she pointed to the other chair. "Sit down and I'll tell you my plan."

Chapter 4

"W ell, what do we do?" Rebekka asked.

Mrs. Sampson took another sip of her coffee and smiled at Rebekka over the rim. "First of all, we take a buggy out to the Strand farm, return the horse, and pick up your things."

"But what about Adolph?"

"By the time we get out there, he should be out in the fields with spring planting. When did you say Mr. and Mrs. Strand are coming back?"

"Tomorrow, Sunday, on the evening train. And you're right. Adolph is behind in his work, so he'll be pushing hard." Rebekka raised stricken eyes to her benefactress. "I don't ever want to see him again."

"I know, my dear." Mrs. Sampson patted Rebekka's hands, clenched on the tablecloth. "That's the beauty of my idea. This way you can return the horse. Adolph is such that he'd probably turn you in for stealing the animal."

"Oh, no. He wouldn't." Rebekka shoved herself to her feet with such fury, the chair rocked behind her. She stormed across the kitchen and back. "Yes, he would. Let's go. I need my shoes and other things so I can go talk with Mr. Larson."

"And I'll be right behind you. You won't get any resistance from him with me along. I know a thing or two about what's going on in this town that just might come in handy right about now."

Rebekka whirled from her pacing and stopped at Mrs. Sampson's side. "You are a jewel among thousands. I can't wait to begin."

"Well, you wash up those dishes while I go get a team at the livery. Then we'll be on our way." Mrs. Sampson paused at the door. "And Rebekka, remember, I'm behind you all the way."

The young woman tried to smile through the film that suddenly covered her eyes but sniffed instead.

The drive out to the Strand farm passed quickly as the two women used the time to get to know each other better. Instead of a wagon, they rode in the comfort of a well-sprung buggy with a flashy chestnut horse trotting between the shafts. The horse that had brought Rebekka to town kept pace behind the buggy, shaking its head now and again at the lead rope.

As they drew nearer, Rebekka slipped into silence. The sight of the house in the distance sent terror coursing from her toes to the top of her head and back down again at breakneck speed. She could feel the fear gnawing at her stomach. What if he was up at the house? She couldn't even bear to use his name.

Mrs. Sampson kept the reins in one hand and used the other to pat Rebekka on the knee. "Now, now. This'll be all over in just a few minutes. There's no need to be afraid. I just know our Father will make this go easy."

Rebekka couldn't force an answer from her dry throat if her life depended upon it.

But for the creaking of the windmill above the well house, the farm lay silent in the sunshine. Rebekka watched the windows carefully to see if the dog's barking brought anyone to peer out. As soon as the dog realized that Rebekka rode in the buggy, he yipped and leaped in apology. *At least the dog likes me,* Rebekka thought, bringing a smile to her quivering lips.

Liking you is just the problem, her inner voice remonstrated with her other thoughts. *If he hadn't liked you so much . . .* Rebekka turned to Mrs. Sampson. "Why don't we pull up at the barn and I'll take the horse inside. Then we can go to the house."

Ten minutes later they were out the door and trotting back down the lane. Rebekka allowed herself both a prayer and a sigh of relief. With her personal items stuffed into a carpetbag and her school things in a box she found on the back porch, she dared breathe in a breath of freedom.

"Maybe I should have left them a letter or something." She looked over her shoulder at the slumbering farm.

"You can always mail them one." Mrs. Sampson flicked the reins over the chestnut's back and he picked up the pace. "I know what I'd like to tell them."

"Ja, I know."

"I just wish there were some way to . . . to . . ."

"Get even?"

"No, I mean, yes." Rebekka paused and drew in a deep breath. "I mean, there should be some way to punish him for what he did and to keep him from doing so again."

"I learned a long time ago that the best revenge is letting God handle the situation. There's a verse, 'Vengeance is mine . . . saith the Lord,' and since He sees more than we do, I'd kinda rather let Him dole out the punishment."

Rebekka thought awhile on the widow's words. "But it seems He takes so long to go about it."

"That's true." Widow Sampson flicked the reins again. "Git up there now. We got plenty important business to tend to."

Widow Sampson looped the reins around the whip pole and descended to the ground in time to lift the box out of the back of the buggy. After tying the horse, the women made their way into the boardinghouse and carried Rebekka's things upstairs to her room.

Rebekka felt herself smiling at the curtains billowing in the fresh breeze. I *already think of this as my room,* she thought in amazement. After two years of moving from home to home, she hadn't thought of any place as her own in a long time.

Mrs. Sampson bustled back out of the room and left Rebekka to redress and redo her hair. Staring in the mirror, Rebekka let her mind wander. Not since she was little had she had a room of her own. After her father started drowning his sorrows in the bottle at the local saloon, she and her mother had been moved from pillar to post with never a place to call their own. And rarely a moment's peace.

But at one time, she'd had a room with a quilt and rug and bright white curtains and a picture of Jesus on the wall. Jesus with the lambs. Rebekka laid her brush back on the dresser. Back at her grandmother's house, she'd had a real home. Back in her grandmother's house, life had been altogether different.

She wound the braid into a scroll at the base of her skull and pushed in the pins to secure it. After dampening a finger, she smoothed back the tendrils about her face that resisted confinement. Now she must present herself to Mr. Larson as her true self.

The old-maid schoolteacher who couldn't—she amended the thought, *wouldn't stay with the Strands any longer.* And she wouldn't, nay, couldn't tell him why.

The two women climbed back up in the buggy with nary a word

between them. Mrs. Sampson slapped the reins over the horse's back and clucked him forward. They turned right on Main Street and trotted past the mercantile, the Lutheran church, and the doctor's dispensary. Mr. Larson lived up on the bluff overlooking the Missouri River. The horse dug in its feet to gain footing on the grade.

"He should be home for dinner about now. Good a time as any to be the bearer of good news."

"Good news?"

"Ja, you're still here." Mrs. Sampson tightened the reins and tied them around the whipstock as soon as the horse stopped. "And you're only asking for a permanent place to live. Not too big a request, considering."

"But . . . but, I can't tell him what really happened."

"No need. Just tell him what you want." She climbed down from the buggy and tied the horse to the rail fence. An apple tree in full bloom filled the air with the fragrance of spring and spread protective arms over the rope swing hung from its branch. A rag doll leaned against the trunk as if comforted by the support.

Rebekka paused at the picket gate. Two of the Larson children attended her school and she knew there were two more at home. How could she talk to the father with his children around?

Mrs. Sampson took Rebekka's arm and led her up to the steps. "Don't be afraid. You have nothing to fear."

Ja, sure. Rebekka felt like ripping her arm from the firm clasp and running back down the road. What would she say if he asked her why? She'd never learned to lie. It was a sin, remember. Her mother had sent her to bed without any supper when she told just a little white fib. What would she say?

She tucked a stray wisp of hair back into the severe coil and squared her shoulders. After one last glance at the woman beside her, Rebekka raised her hand and tapped on the door.

The door opened and Mrs. Larson greeted them with a wide smile. "Come in, come in. Why, if I'd knowed you were coming, we could have set another two places at the table for dinner." She wiped her hands on her skirt-length white apron and gestured them toward the sitting room. "Can I get you some coffee? We'll be having dessert in just a minute. Lars, look who's here, Miss Stenesrude and Widow Sampson."

After exchanging a conspiratorial glance, Rebekka and Mrs. Sampson followed their hostess. Nothing had changed. Give Mrs. Larson a moment and look out. When she started talking it took stronger hearts than theirs to stop her.

She bustled them into sitting on the horsehair sofa in the sitting room and met herself going out again.

"I . . . I need to talk with Mr. Larson," Rebekka called to the retreating back. The woman bustled on.

"Whew," Mrs. Sampson drew the back of her hand across her forehead as if to wipe away a flood of perspiration. She leaned back against the stiff sofa and turned to warm Rebekka with a smile. "Can't say as I ever am prepared when I see Elmira after a time. She talks faster than a tornado spins." She kept her voice to a whisper.

Rebekka clamped her bottom lip between her teeth and forced herself to sit perfectly erect, her feet primly together, her shoulders back and chin high. That was the only way to keep from turning into a mound of mush. Surely this couldn't be worse than facing a class of twenty brand-new students, ranging in age from five to fifteen. She bit her lip. Yes, it could. What if she had to lie? Why, oh, why couldn't Adolph keep his hands and lascivious thoughts to himself? Only with sternest self-control did she keep herself from shuddering.

Mr. Lars Larson sported the sunburned face and pure white forehead of a man who spent his days in the blazing Dakota sunshine. No ruler could have drawn a more perfect line than the one his hatband had done, dividing his face. He wore the sober look of a proper Norwegian upon learning that women were calling upon him in his professional capacity as school superintendent.

"Now, what can I do for you ladies?" he asked after all the proper greetings were exchanged.

A movement at the door caught Rebekka's attention. Two shining faces with smiles fit to crack a rock, peered around the corner. The girl, braids pulling her hair into some semblance of order, waved and then hid her giggle behind her hands.

"Come, children, say hello to your teacher and then go about your chores." Mr. Larson shot an apologetic glance at the women sitting on his sofa and beckoned the children. Two smaller replicas tagged behind the boy and girl who were her students.

"Hello, Inga and Ernie." Rebekka reached out her hands to clasp those of the towheaded children and draw them to her side. "Maybe you could introduce me to your brother and sister."

"This is Mary and Johnny. They're twins." Inga took over as the oldest.

"They're babies. They don't go to school like us big kids." Ernie puffed out his skinny chest, visible under the straps of his faded overalls.

The two little ones clung to the chair where their father sat. When Rebekka greeted them, they each stuck one finger in their mouths and ducked their heads in perfect unison.

"They always do everything the same." Ernie turned his serious blue-eyed gaze on his teacher. "Ma says that's 'cause they was borned at the same time."

Rebekka nodded. She dredged up every bit of schoolmarm control to keep from ordering the children out to play so the adults could talk.

Mr. Larson must have sensed her feelings for he patted the twins on the bottom of their matching overalls and sent them out of the room. "Inga, Ernie, enough now. You go help your ma."

The children filed out of the room, sending smiles over their shoulders.

Mr. Larson turned as they left. "And Inga, close the door behind you."

Rebekka breathed a sigh of relief at his consideration. All of a sudden, the coming interview didn't seem quite as frightening. Surely a man as considerate of his children as this would be sympathetic to her plight.

"Now, you want to talk with me. How can I help you?" He looked from Rebekka to Mrs. Sampson and back.

The silence deepened as the discomfort level in the room rose. Rebekka looked toward Mrs. Sampson and received a nod of encouragement. "I . . . I—" She pictured herself in front of a classroom of students and took a deep breath. "I cannot remain at the Strands' any longer. The situation there is totally untenable and I must have another place to live." The words gained strength and purpose as they followed one another, starting at a stagger and ending in a march.

Mr. Larson leaned back in his chair, rubbing the line of demarcation between summer and winter on his forehead. "Well, you know, we've always done things for the schoolteacher this way. He or she, you in this case, moves from home to home throughout the school year. We excuse those folks who absolutely can't afford to feed the teacher or who don't have room for one."

"I know." Rebekka lifted her chin a mite higher.

"What else can we do? Now, if you were married, you'd be living in your husband's house and then there wouldn't be no problem."

Rebekka bit her lip on a retort to that nugget of information.

"Just what's the problem with finishing out your stay at the Strands'?"

Rebekka refused to cringe at the blunt question. Instead, she looked Mr. Larson straight in the face and answered, "I'd rather not say." Now she knew what a witness must feel like in court.

Out of the corner of her eye Rebekka could see Mrs. Sampson straighten herself, an act that reminded her of a hen all fluffed up and ready to attack anyone who disturbs her chicks.

Mr. Larson raised a hand. "Please don't think I'm not concerned about this. I am only trying to get to the bottom of a problem." Mrs. Sampson cleared her throat.

Rebekka felt a burst of strength, as if she were inhaling confidence. "We have worked together now for the good of Willowford's children for nearly two years. Wouldn't you agree that it's been a productive two years, Mr. Larson?"

"Well, of course."

"Wouldn't you like to continue the progress that we've made?" Without giving him time for a response, she sailed on. "At this time, we have all the school-age children in the district enrolled in school and two of our eldest are preparing for college. Now, wouldn't you say those are major accomplishments?"

"Yes, I—"

Mrs. Sampson leaned back just a trifle.

"I would be sorry to see the education of Willowford's children suffer even the smallest of disruptions, wouldn't you?" Rebekka asked.

Mr. Larson nodded.

"I hear there's a shortage of teachers coming out of Normal School the last couple of years." Mrs. Sampson nodded sagely. "The folks of Willowford do appreciate having a trained teacher over in the schoolhouse." While unspoken, her "for a change" rang through the quiet of the room.

Mr. Larson rubbed his forehead again. "Now, look. This is the way we've always done it. And it's worked. Now, why should we change?"

"Remember that incident one night last summer?" Mrs. Sampson tossed the question out, casually, as if she were pitching a pebble into a pond.

Mr. Larson's lower face matched his forehead. He closed his eyes. "Oh, my."

"Now, the ways I see it, Miss Stenesrude would be much closer to the school, were she to live in my house. Beings we're just across the creek from the schoolhouse."

"But we have no money."

"And that way she could go over on cold mornings to start the stove earlier. Keep Willowford's children warmer, you might say." Only a groan rose from the other chair.

"You can be sure I would do my part for the children of my community and give you a real good rate. In fact, it might be that Miss Stenesrude would be willing to help me out some, to help pay her expenses, you know."

Mr. Larson leaned forward. "I'd have to clear this with the rest of the school board, you realize."

"Like you did the well?" Mrs. Sampson smiled, but the whisper penetrated to the bone.

"I take it this would be agreeable to you?" Mr. Larson turned to Rebekka. At her nod, he continued. "When would you like me to go with you to pick up your things at Strands'?"

"We've already done that," Mrs. Sampson said, "I know you won't regret this, Lars. You've made a wise decision and the fewer people who know about this, the better. Don't you agree?"

Mr. Larson mumbled something as he pushed himself to his feet. "Let me see what is keeping Elmira with that coffee."

Rebekka breathed a sigh of pure relief. She hadn't had to lie. But on the way home, she was surely going to ask Mrs. Sampson what had happened last summer.

⚶

By Monday morning Rebekka felt like she'd lived at the widow's boardinghouse all her life. While she'd had a nightmare on Saturday night, Sunday night she slept through and woke up to face the new day with joy and a sense of adventure.

Rebekka felt a smile tug at the corners of her mouth as she lay in bed relishing the peace and loveliness surrounding her. While dancing in the early morning breeze, the sheer curtains struggled against the ties that looped them back. When she planted her feet on the braided rug, she resisted the urge to dance along with the curtains. Stretching her arms over her head to banish the last yawn, she crossed to the window and knelt to place her crossed arms on the sill.

"This is the day that the Lord hath made, I will rejoice and be glad in it." Her verse was certainly easier to live up to today than it had been in the days past. "Thank You, Father, for bringing me here to live. It's been so long since I felt like I had a real home. What would it be like to have a home of my own?" She thought of the Larsons, their fine home on the hill, and their towheaded brood. Would she ever have a home like that? Was there a man out there somewhere who would invite her to share his home? Who would love her with the kind of love Christ talked about? Whom she would love the same way?

A robin pipped his early morning love song to the heavens from the tree in the corner of the backyard. Rebekka searched the branches until she saw him, his red breast puffed out and beak open wide. "Hope you find her, Mr. Robin," she whispered. "Everyone needs that perfect mate." She swallowed the lost feeling that crept over her and pushed herself to her feet.

"How silly, mooning around like that." She scolded herself all the way through her morning wash and even while brushing her hair. Long, wavy strands that shaded from wren brown to deep sienna snapped in the electricity from her brush, creating a cloud about her head that reached halfway down her back.

She smiled at the heart-shaped face in the mirror. What would it be like to wear her hair free but for two combs to catch it back from her face? She laughed at the sight of her hands trying to harness all that wildness. What was the matter with her this morning? She wet the brush and slicked the unruly strands straight back and into their usual braid and the braid into its coil at the base of her head.

She checked the mirror again. There now, the schoolmarm was back in control where she should be. The old-maid schoolmarm who would always teach other peoples' children to the best of her ability.

She quickly made up her bed and, picking up the slop jar, made her way downstairs for breakfast.

The feeling of anticipation returned as she crossed the bridge that spanned Bryde Creek. The creek flowed full and brown, swelled with runoff from the spring rains. At the sound of her feet tapping on the planks, Rebekka gave a little skip and four quick heel smacks to add to the stream's spring song. Soon the summer would be here and what would she do then?

She continued the thought. Eight more days of school and then the big picnic. Everyone was already having trouble studying and the older boys had left weeks earlier to help with spring planting. Other years she had returned to stay with her mother in Minnesota, but since her mother died, she had no family—no immediate family that is. Somewhere she might have relatives on her father's side, but no one knew for sure. Her mother had a sister somewhere, but they had lost touch through the years of her father's dragging them from pillar to post and back again.

"And that's what being married gets you," she warned the creek. "So stay the way you are." Her heels clicked a rhythm of their own as she headed on toward the schoolhouse. She looked around to see if anyone had heard or seen her—talking to the creek no less. Surely they'd think she'd been addled by the sun or something. Definitely not a good example for a teacher to set.

She looked over her shoulder, a grin peeking out around her admonishments. So was the creek male or female and was it really single? Or would you call it a marriage when two creeks flowed together and then into the river? She shook her head. Maybe she had been addled by something. Or maybe she'd been around her pupils too long. Those were the kinds of questions she encouraged from them.

She'd written the instructions for the first lesson of the day on the blackboard before some pupils arrived giggling at the door. Rebekka put all thoughts of her own questions out of her mind and concentrated on her pupils. She checked the small watch she wore pinned to her plain white blouse. Ten minutes until school began. "Mith Thtenthrude," a small charmer with two missing front teeth lisped. "Our cat had kittenth."

Rebekka squatted down to be on eye level. "How many did she have?"

Emily wrinkled her forehead and began raising fingers until she showed four on one hand and one on the other. "Five."

"Very good. Is she taking good care of them?"

"Yeth. Thee had them in Bernie'th bed." She clapped her hands over her mouth to stifle the giggle. Her blue eyes sparkled, and when Rebekka laughed with her, they both looked back to see Bernie plunking his lunch pail down on his desk. Emily whispered between her fingers. "Bernie wath mad."

Rebekka rose to her feet and checked her watch again. "Bernie, would you be so kind as to ring the warning bell?"

Bernie nodded his pleasure and scampered out to the cloakroom, where the heavy rope hung from the bell tower. As the bell pealed its warning across the town, she could hear the children shouting and laughing as they ran toward the school.

Yes, this would be another high-spirited day and there was so much she wished to teach them before the end of the year. She waited for them at the door as they lined up, boys on one side and girls on the other, starting with the youngest in front and ending with the oldest. The boys' line was regrettably short since all those over twelve were helping their fathers in the fields.

"Bernie, the final bell." She waited while the tones rang out again. It was precisely eight o'clock. "Elizabeth, will you lead the morning prayer?" At the girl's nod, Rebekka opened the Bible she carried. "Today we will read from Psalm Twenty-three. 'The Lord is my shepherd; I shall not want.' Now, let us repeat that together." All the voices raised in unison at the familiar verse. At Rebekka's nod, Elizabeth bowed her head and waited for the shuffling to cease. Her musical voice joined with the bird choruses from the trees planted on each side of the school.

"Father in Heaven, we thank Thee for this day. Thank Thee that we can go to school and learn so many things. Please help us to do our best." Elizabeth paused, then finished swiftly. "And let everyone come to the picnic. Amen."

Rebekka rolled her lips together to keep from smiling. She and every child there knew Elizabeth was hoping that James Johnson would be in attendance. Elizabeth and James had been making eyes at each other for the last year.

"Thorlief, will you lead the flag salute?" At his answering grin, she turned and led her charges into the schoolroom.

When all the feet ceased shuffling, the boy's voice began, "I pledge allegiance to the flag . . ." At the finish, they all took their seats and folded their hands on their desktops.

Rebekka sat down at the piano and sounded the opening chords for "America the Beautiful." As the voices rose in song, she felt shivers run down her back. The children sang so wonderfully.

After the singing, she walked to the front of the room. "Today we'll start with reading. Take out your books, please."

By the end of the day, Rebekka felt like she'd been whipped through the eye of a hurricane twice. After the last child departed, she had yet to sweep the floor and wash the blackboards. These were all chores the older boys did when they were in attendance, so she missed their presence doubly. She also needed to work on her lesson plans for the rest of the week.

When she finally closed the schoolhouse door, she sank down on the steps and wrapped her arms around her knees. At least she didn't have to walk two miles home again like she had done for the last month. And other places had been farther. She breathed in deeply of the soft air, content to be right where she was at that very moment.

Rebekka was as ready as her pupils were for the school picnic.

They'd planned games and contests for every age group from the three-year-old race to the horseshoe pitching for the older men, with the school board providing awards. Everyone in town and the surrounding area was invited.

That Saturday dawned with a thundershower, but by ten o'clock, the sun shone brightly and folks began to gather. Trestle tables had been set out and they groaned under the array of food brought by the women.

Rebekka stood on the steps and surveyed the colorful crowd. If numbers were any indication, this would be the very best school picnic that Willowford had ever seen. Only one cloud floated on her horizon—would Adolph Strand have the gall to appear? She checked every wagon and buckboard that drove up and tied up in the grove down by the creek.

"Anything else you need?" Mr. Larson appeared at her side.

"No, nothing. Just enjoying the excitement. The children have been looking forward to this day nearly as much as Christmas." Rebekka returned a wave from a newly arrived family. "Thank you for the prizes you brought. And also for the extra gifts. It means so much to the little ones to be part of the school program."

"Well, you met my two. They'd be crushed if everyone got something and not them, so I brought plenty. We'll save the leftovers for next year." He picked a stalk of grass and nibbled on the succulent stem. "Ah," he muttered as he chewed the stalk and spit out the tough section. "Umm," he started as he studied the toe of his dusty boot.

"Yes?"

He looked up at the tops of the trees bordering the creek. "There . . . ah . . . been any problems, I mean anyone hanging around or anything?"

Rebekka could recognize the flush creeping up Mr. Larson's neck because it matched the one on her own. "No, no problem. And thank you for your concern." She bent down to answer a question from one of her young students, grateful for the distraction.

When she stood up again, Mr. Larson was striding across the schoolyard. *Bless you,* she thought. *You really care and yet it is so hard for you to show it.*

By late afternoon parents were loading tired and even some sleeping children into the wagons, gathering up their things, and heading home to do evening chores. If the enthusiasm of those departing meant anything, the picnic had indeed been the success Rebekka dreamed.

Now it was time to close the school for the summer. Since several of the women had already helped clean while the children were running three-legged and sack races, the building had the smell and sound of summer slumber. The last remaining pupils policed the yard, cleaning up every scrap of paper, and then charged off to their homes.

"Bye, Miss Stenesrude. See you in the fall. Have a good summer." The calls went back and forth. Mr. Larson locked the door for the final time and pocketed the key.

"What are you figuring to do this summer?" he asked as they stopped at the rail fence bounding the schoolyard.

"I don't rightly know, besides helping Mrs. Sampson, that is." She looked up at him with a smile. "But I'm sure the good Lord knows. He promised to provide."

"Ja, that's right." He tipped his hat. "Be seein' you then." He started off, then turned. "You want a ride back to town?"

"No, thank you. I like the walk." She waved him off and, after picking up her bag loaded with books and papers, ambled toward the boardinghouse. When she paused on the bridge and looked down, the creek had retreated to its summertime ramblings, burbling over stones and babbling around tree roots. The song it sang seemed to promise good things ahead.

Even though she was tired from the rigorous day, Rebekka found herself smiling with the stream and singing its song on her way home.

"There's a letter for you," Mrs. Sampson called when Rebekka walked in the door.

Chapter 5

"Next stop, Willowford."

The conductor called. *Next stop, home,* thought Rebekka as she stared out the window, trying to catch a glimpse of a familiar landmark. Two months was a long time to have been gone. She leaned her head back against the seat and thought of all that had happened since she had opened the letter . . . the letter from her grandmother, her father's mother.

She still couldn't believe how they had found her. And now she had family. She, who had no one, suddenly had a grandmother, an aunt, three cousins, and various other in-laws and almost in-laws. People in Minneapolis certainly did live differently than her friends in Willowford. Why, she'd never seen the contraptions called horseless carriages, electric lights, and indoor privies. Granted, she'd read about those things in newspapers, but now she'd seen them with her own eyes.

She brought herself back to the present and peered out the window, checking if she could see the Missouri yet. Instead she saw smoke.

Smoke across the prairie, as far as she could see! Prairie fire! Fire between here and Willowford. Which way was the wind blowing? Would the train be trapped? The thoughts raced through her mind like flames driven before a gale-force wind.

"No worry, folks," the conductor announced in his sonorous voice. "The wind is coming from the east, blowing due west, so we're in no danger."

Unless the wind changes, Rebekka let her thoughts drift to the cataclysm on the prairie. While the train slowed down, she leaned forward, as if she could encourage it to forge ahead. What was happening in Willowford? There was nothing to stop the fire between here and there. She'd seen the Willowford Volunteer Fire Department practice. Had they put their skills to use?

As the train covered the remaining miles, the prairie on each side of the tracks lay charred and blackened. Some fence posts still smoldered, and here and there a haystack sent tendrils of smoke skyward. Farm buildings off to the north lay in an oasis of green where the farmer had set a backfire to save his home. Plowed firebreaks kept the rampaging inferno from gobbling up another farm. A third lay in smoking ruins.

"They was some good, the soddies like I lived in as a child," one of the passengers said. "Prairie fire burnt right on over us. All we had to eat that year was potatoes. Good thing the livestock lived in a soddie barn, too. I'll never forget us runnin' to herd the cows and chickens inside."

Rebekka shuddered. But people didn't live in soddies anymore, usually.

Smoking piles of animal dung dotted a pasture. She hated to look in case there were also dead animals lying around, but so far she didn't see any.

The train whistle sent its haunting call ahead of them. Rebekka leaned her forehead against the grimy window. The feeling of relief at the sight of buildings still standing caused a lump to rise in her throat. But where was the creek, the trees that lived along its bank? And that smoking ruin she could barely see for the tears streaming down her cheeks. The schoolhouse lay in smoldering rubble.

Her schoolhouse. All the books for which they'd saved and scrimped. The flag, the bell . . . had she left any of her personal things in the desk? She thought of the shelves of books donated for a library someday. All gone.

She drew a handkerchief from her bag and wiped her eyes. As the train crossed the railroad bridge over the creek, she understood why it was hard to see from a distance. The men had cut the trees to use the creek as a firebreak. The trunks and limbs not under water still smoldered. The men of the town leaned on shovels or tossed dirt on stubborn patches. Black with soot, they stared at the train, their weariness evident in the drooped shoulders and slackjawed faces.

Rebekka blew her nose. She couldn't cry anymore now. At least they'd saved the town. They could rebuild the school. But until then, where would they meet? The church? School was due to start in three short weeks. What would they use for books?

Her mind raced ahead as she stepped down on the station platform and thanked the conductor for his assistance. Had anyone been injured? Guilt stabbed her as all she thought about was her school. Buildings could be rebuilt, but what if someone had died or was severely burned? Were the children all right?

She set off down the street to Widow Sampson's boardinghouse. Men congregated at the saloon where the owner had rolled out a keg and was handing out free beer.

"Miss Stenesrude, Miss Stenesrude." A young boy, blackened and unrecognizable, came running across the dusty street. "Did ya see? The schoolhouse burnt right down."

"Yes, I saw. Is everyone all right?"

"Ja, just some burns from blowing stuff. And everybody's coughing. You never had no tiling hurt like breathing smoke. Pa says we'll prob'ly start school in the church until they can build a new school."

"Thank you, Kenny." Rebekka felt relieved she'd finally figured out who her bearer of bad tidings was.

"Can I help you with your bag?" The boy fell in step beside her. "I'm plenty strong."

With a flash of trepidation, Rebekka relinquished her bag to the boy's sooty hand. How would she get the soot off the handle? She pushed the thought back as unchristian. Her "Thank you" sounded more fervent because of her doubts.

"Ah, my dear, I am so glad you are returned and safe through all this." Mrs. Sampson wiped her hands on her apron and grasped one of Rebekka's in both of hers. "How was your family? Ain't it awful about the school? But thank the good Lord, He spared the town. They was all ready to send the women and children to the other side of the river by boats and the ferry, but we was fightin' the fire right alongside the men."

Rebekka felt a stab of guilt. She should have been here helping. "Were they able to save anything from the school?"

Mrs. Sampson just shook her head. "And no one's been out to the farmers yet to see how they fared. We just came home and washed up. My hair's still damp." She patted the coronet of braids she wore.

"Have you had any new boarders?" Rebekka asked from halfway up the stairs.

"Nah, your room is still the same one. You make yourself at home and I'll have the coffee ready shortly. Mrs. Knutson went over to her shop to check and make sure everything is all right there. We'll have supper soon's I can set things out. If you still would like to help me, we need to wash everything down tomorrow to get rid of the soot. Like spring cleaning all over again. I closed up the rooms afore I left to help on the fire line, so this house ain't bad as some."

Rebekka shuddered. The smell of smoke permeated *everything* inside and out, and the odor made her eyes water. What they needed now was a good rain to wash things clean again.

That night she fell asleep with her windows wide open and the breeze trying to blow away the fire's residue. How good it felt to be home, in spite of the fire. But what would she do about school?

In the morning the three women were aproned and wearing kerchiefs tied over their heads to protect their hair as they dragged the rugs out to the line for a good beating, washed and hung out the curtains, and scrubbed down every surface in the house. Since she was the tallest, Rebekka stood on a stool to wash the outsides of the windows.

"Good afternoon, Miss Stenesrude," Mr. Larson called as he opened the picket gate and strode up the walk. "Seems everyone in town is doing the same thing today. Scrubbing and counting our blessings. Good to see you back."

"Good to be back. Although I wasn't too excited about my welcome." She climbed down from her stool and wiped her hands on her apron. "What can I do for you?"

"Could you come to a school board meeting tonight at the church at seven?"

"Of course."

"Good. I have two more members to call on. I'll see you then." He turned and strode back to his horse. "See you tonight."

The meeting that night had one item on the agenda. How would they get the money to rebuild the schoolhouse?

Within a week the bank had loaned the school district enough money to begin the building. Rebekka spent a good part of every day driving the buggy to the outlying farms to invite the people to a school raising.

"You mean like a barn raising?" one woman asked.

"Just like that." Rebekka nodded. "Plan on the second Saturday in September. Most people will be done harvesting by then, so we'll make it into a school building and end of harvest celebration. If enough people turn out, we should be able to frame the walls and put on the roof by Sunday night."

"Count on us."

Rebekka missed only one farm and that was intentional. As she drove by the Strands', she kept her eyes straight ahead. But ignoring the goosebumps chasing each other up and down her back wasn't as easy as looking the other way. Why did she feel that the whole situation wasn't resolved yet? She hadn't even heard hide nor hair of Adolph. She tried to put a lid on her worry box. "Remember, you ninny, that God says He watches over us like a hen with her chicks. And you know how fierce that little hen can be." The horse flicked his ears at her voice.

The lumber came in on the train, and the townspeople hauled it in their wagons to the school site. Rebekka walked among the stacked lumber piles, inhaling the scent of freshly milled timbers and siding. Wooden kegs of nails, crates of window glass, and the sawhorses belonging to Lars Larson lay in readiness. The flat river rocks used for support under posts and beams had been measured and placed in the proper positions.

Off to the side, the cast-iron bell salvaged from the burned building rested, cleaned and repainted and ready to lift into the new tower. Rebekka stopped at the bell and tapped it with the toe of her boot. A hollow thunk made her smile. Like everyone or everything, the bell needed to be hung in the right position to make music. "Soon," she promised the inert object. "Soon you'll be calling the children to school again." She turned in place, taking in all the supplies, ready for the morning. All that was needed were the people.

The hammering and sawing started about the time the first rooster crowed in Willowford. Rebekka bounded out of bed and rushed through her morning toilet as if she were afraid she might miss out on something. Downstairs, Mrs. Sampson was already taking three apple pies out of the oven.

"How can we find room on the table?" Rebekka moved bowls of food around to make room for the steaming pans. "You trying to feed all the builders yourself?"

"Nah. Just doing my share."

Rebekka dished herself a bowl of oatmeal from the kettle on the back of the stove. "You'd be up there nailing if they'd let you."

"Ja, I would. But since they'd drum an old woman like me . . ." Rebekka gave a decidedly unladylike snort. Mrs. Sampson gave her a look and then continued, "Off the roof, I want to make sure the workers come back the next day to finish the job. Our children need that school."

"And I need my job." Rebekka poured a dollop of molasses on her cereal, then some milk, and sat down to eat. "But what are we going to do for books and desks? The library? Oh, and our piano?"

"Won't the insurance cover some of that?"

"I hope. But it all depends on how much the rebuilding costs. I sent a letter to the state teachers' association requesting their help and Mr. Larson contacted the State Board of Education. But all that takes time."

"We used to have the parents pay for their children's books. So there still might be books in people's homes that can be used. If you tell everyone to bring any books they have at home, you'll have something to start with." Mrs. Sampson lifted the full teakettle off the stove and filled the dishpan in the cast-iron sink.

"Thanks. I'll start passing the word today. Do you have someone to help carry all this over to the schoolyard?"

"I'm picking up the wagon at the livery at ten. Then Mrs. Knutson and I'll go around to some of the other houses to help them. I'm bringing my washtubs for the lemonade."

Jude Weinlander let his horse drink from the river's edge. He leaned his forearms on the saddle horn and stared upriver. The town lay shimmering in the September heat, and even from this distance he could hear the pounding of hammers.

He stared across the blackened prairie, where shoots of green could be seen poking up through the ashes toward the sunlight. Drying goldenrod nodded in the breeze across the river, where leaves already sported the tinges of fall. But on this side, all lay desolate.

When his horse, Prince, raised its head, ears pricked toward the sound of building, Jude nudged the animal forward. "That's the way we'll head then." He spoke for the first time since he mounted up, just before sunrise. The horse flicked his ears as if truly interested in what was being said. "Hope you know what you're doing." The horse snorted and broke into a trot. When he raised his head and whinnied, a horse answered from the town ahead.

Jude sat on his horse at the edge of the beehive of activity. Floor joists and flooring were already in place and different groups were framing up the walls. The north wall stood while men nailed the plate in place. Hammers pounding, saws buzzing, people laughing and swapping stories, children running and laughing along a creek where the willows had been cut for the firebreak—it looked more like a party than a building site.

Across the creek, Jude could see the town. He strained to read the sign on the train station—WILLOWFORD. He shrugged. Good a place as any. Maybe they could use another hand on the building.

He watched the busy scene to determine who was in charge. A tall man, fedora pulled low on his forehead, seemed to be answering questions and keeping his laborers busy. Jude stepped from his horse and tipped his hat back before searching in his saddlebags for hammer and pigskin gloves. Before leaving his mount, he loosened the saddle cinch and wrapped the reins around a willow stump.

Two barefoot, overalls-clad youngsters charged by him, their speed outclassed only by the volume of their shouts.

"Need anything to drink?" A tall woman dressed in a white blouse and ankle-length serge skirt moved from helper to helper offering drinks from a bucket on her arm.

"You got something stronger than that lemonade?" One of the sweating hammer wielders asked.

"Now, you know better than that." The woman grinned, changing her face from plain to pretty. Auburn highlights glinted from hair imprisoned in a coil of braids at the back of her head. Springy tendrils of hair framed her heart-shaped face in spite of her determined efforts to tuck them back into their prison.

As if feeling his gaze, she turned and stared straight at him. With one hand she brushed back a lock of hair before going on to the next man to offer him a drink.

He watched the way she moved about the yard, her long-legged stride, free of feminine artifice. Funny, he hadn't noticed something like the way she moved, since, well, since . . . He clamped a lid on the memories of his other life. Nothing mattered now but the next job . . . the next town . . . the next meal. And maybe working here for a few hours would at least give him that.

He kept his eye on the man in charge, following him around the corner of the building before getting his attention. "Ah, sir."

The man waved at a man nailing boards in place on a wall frame and then strode over to answer another's question.

Jude paused by a man busily sawing boards laid across the sawhorses. "Who is the man in charge here?" he asked.

"Ah, that'd be Lars Larson, the man getting a drink from the schoolmarm."

"Thanks." Jude tipped his hat and, stepping across a couple of beams, made his way around the building. So that's who she was, the schoolmarm. "Mr. Larson." He walked closer. "Mr. Larson."

Lars Larson turned from a laughing comment exchanged with the tall woman Jude had noticed before. "Ja?" At the sight of a stranger, he offered his hand. "I'm Lars Larson. What can I do for you?"

"I wondered if maybe you could use another hand." Jude concentrated on keeping his gaze from swinging to the woman. He forced himself to look Mr. Larson in the eye instead.

"You know how to use a hammer?"

Jude nodded, his mouth set in a firm line.

"I can't pay you. This is a community project. The school burnt in a prairie fire a few weeks ago." Mr. Larson studied the man in front of him. "But there'll be plenty of food, if'n that appeals to you."

Jude nodded. "That'll be fine."

"You go on and join that crew on the front wall."

Jude tipped his hat to Mr. Larson and then to the woman standing off to the side with a slight smile on her face. "Ma'am." He turned and pulled on his gloves while crossing the schoolyard.

As he reached the men raising the wall, he drew his hammer from its place in his belt in the back on the right side.

"Who is he?" Rebekka stared after the man. She turned to Mr. Larson, who shrugged.

"Just a drifter, I imagine. At least he'll get a good feed for his labors." Mr. Larson took another sip from the dipper and wiped his mouth with the back of his hand. "Thank you, Miss Stenesrude. That lemonade tastes mighty fine."

He didn't even say his name and I heard everything they said. Rebekka allowed her thoughts to drift as she continued around the building with the lemonade bucket. Again she saw and felt the shock of his gaze. Did she know him from somewhere else? She tried to think. No, she'd remember someone with a gaze so summer-sky blue. Eyes so blue they seemed to pierce like shards of ice on a winter day. Now why did she think of winter? Today when the sun was so hot that she'd had to wipe her face with a handkerchief twice already.

She returned to the washtub to refill her bucket and she felt it again.

How could the gaze from a man she'd never even met before send shivers up and down her spine?

Rebekka handed her half-full bucket to her oldest pupil, reminding her to stay out of the way of the men while they worked, and then she went over to help the women setting up the tables for dinner. From the looks of the groaning boards, no one would go hungry. In fact, there'd be plenty left for supper, too. That way those that didn't have animals to care for could work through until dark.

"Who was that man talking with you and Lars?" Mrs. Sampson paused in the act of cutting her pies.

"I have no idea." Rebekka felt the urge to look over her shoulder again. If she did, she was sure she would see him watching her. "He didn't give his name, just said he knew how to use a hammer."

"Well, he wasn't just blowing smoke. I been watching him. You mark my words, he's used that hammer plenty. Has an air of mystery about him, wouldn't you say? Or maybe it's sadness."

"I wouldn't say at all. I don't know the man and probably never will." Rebekka turned to her friend. "You sure have strange ideas. He's just a drifter."

"I wouldn't be too sure."

Just then someone came up to ask Rebekka a question, so she had no more time to pursue the discussion. But something niggled at her just the same. Who was he?

At the stroke of noon Rebekka rang the triangle, calling everyone to eat. The Reverend Haugen came down off the ladder where he'd been nailing on the upper plate and, after wiping his face on a bright red kerchief, bowed his head. "We thank Thee, O Lord, for the gifts Thou hast given us, for the food the women have prepared, for the progress on our building, and for the protection Thee offers us all. Hear our prayer and now give us strength to continue through the day before us." At the universal "Amen," he raised his hands. "Let's eat."

The men formed two lines and moved down the length of the laden tables, loading their plates as they went. Another row of tables had benches on each side ready for the men to slide first one foot and then the other under the table and sit down. As soon as the men had filled their plates, the women and children did the same.

Rebekka had switched from carrying lemonade to carrying coffee and made her way down the table with a huge pot. At her "Coffee?" the seated men held up the mug from on the table in front of them.

"There's more lemonade, too," she said as she poured coffee and offered praises for jobs well done.

"Coffee?" she said again, stopping just before the stranger. He turned without a word and held up his cup.

Rebekka felt her hand shake as she poured the dark brew. When the cup was full, she raised her gaze to see the man studying her over the rim of the cup. He lifted the steaming mug and, after one swallow, turned and set the cup down. Without a word, smile, thank you, or by your leave, he resumed eating.

Rebekka paused as if giving him a chance to remedy his bad manners. But when he continued to fork potato salad into his mouth without another glance, she stepped to the next man at the table.

"Coffee?" Now her voice shook, too. She cleared her throat and took a tighter grip on the pot holders with which she held the pot. Of all the . . .

She stayed away from him after that—far away—and did the slow burn. What an ingrate. Had his mother not taught him common decency? No manners? Everyone was taught to at least say "Thank you." Weren't they?

Obviously not. She stopped after her last round with the water bucket and gazed up at the new schoolhouse.

As the sun was setting, the men on the roof were nailing the last rafter in place.

"That's it for tonight," Mr. Larson called. "We'll start again at first light. Reverend Haugen has agreed to lead the worship service tomorrow right here so those who want can attend without much of a loss of time. We can use the good Lord's blessing." He waved toward the tables, set now with plates of sandwiches and the leftovers from dinner. "Now, come and help yourselves. These women would be mighty hurt if anyone left here hungry."

Rebekka kneaded the aching muscles of her lower back with her fists. If she had to carry one more coffeepot she was sure her shoulders would come loose from their sockets. She could hear others groaning, too, but everyone laughed off the pains and dug into the food.

Jude pounded in the last nail and, after sticking his hammer back into its usual place, he climbed down the ladder. He pulled off his gloves and tucked them into his back pocket, then crossed to where the men were washing their hands and faces in a row of buckets of water lined up on a bench.

He tipped his hat back and, sloshing water up in cupped hands, he washed his face first, then hands, and finally his arms up to his rolled-back sleeves. He could feel someone watching him but, when he turned around, no one seemed to be paying him any attention. Then why that creepy crawly sensation up his spine? He lifted his hat and ran damp fingers through the waves trapped beneath the hatband. The slash of silver that began at his upper temple on the left side caught a glint from the setting sun.

The glint caught Rebekka's gaze, in spite of her efforts to not look at the man. What was wrong with her? She'd never in her life paid so much attention to one man, and a drifter at that.

After the crowd finished eating, they slowly left the school grounds and headed for their homes. Lars Larson sat down beside Jude on the bench and leaned his elbows on the table. "You sure got a way with that hammer of yours. Been building long?"

Jude shook his head. "Nope, just the last year or so."

"You from these parts?"

"No." Jude cut and levered another bite of pie into his mouth.

"You plannin' on coming back tomorrow?"

"If nobody minds."

"You got a place to stay?" Mr. Larson leaned on his elbows.

"Down by the river'll do."

"You're welcome to my barn. You can put your horse out in the pasture and leave him there long as you want." Mr. Larson swiveled around like he was getting ready to leave. "What'd you say your name was?"

"Jude Weinlander. And I appreciate the offer." Jude accepted a cup of coffee from the woman pouring and thanked her. Then he turned back to Mr. Larson. "Just where is your barn?"

Mr. Larson pointed out his house on the knoll on the other side of Willowford and pushed himself to his feet. "See you in the morning then and thanks for your work on the school today."

Jude nodded. He watched as the man gathered his family into a wagon and drove off. He slapped at a mosquito buzzing around his head and sipped his coffee. This was a good town, he could tell already. The townsfolk made even drifters feel welcome, at least this one who could nail up a wall with the best of them.

He turned and studied the bare bones of the new school. Siding covered most of two walls, the rafters were ready for the nailers, and two men had been splitting cedar shakes to finish the roof. Tomorrow would make a big difference if as many people turned out as today. He inhaled air redolent of freshly sawed wood. Even the ache in his back only added to the contentment. He started to reach in his pocket for a cigar but remembered he didn't even have a nickel to buy one. He'd have to find a paying job pretty soon.

Bedded down on soft hay that night, he thought back again to the day. Glints of auburn off a tall woman's hair and a laugh that floated like music on the air brought a smile to a face that had found little reason to smile in a long while.

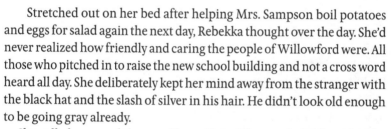

Stretched out on her bed after helping Mrs. Sampson boil potatoes and eggs for salad again the next day, Rebekka thought over the day. She'd never realized how friendly and caring the people of Willowford were. All those who pitched in to raise the new school building and not a cross word heard all day. She deliberately kept her mind away from the stranger with the black hat and the slash of silver in his hair. He didn't look old enough to be going gray already.

She rolled over and thumped her pillow. Who was he? Where had he come from? She could ask Mr. Larson tomorrow. Sure, just go up and say, "Mr. Larson, I saw you talking with that stranger. Tell me his life history." Even the thought of such outrageous actions sent the heat flaming up her neck.

If she waited long enough, Mrs. Sampson would find out plenty. If she had the patience to wait. A mighty big word, "if." Would he be back tomorrow?

Chapter 6

"Y ou think he'll be back today?" Rebekka asked.

"Who'll be back?" Mrs. Sampson removed a pot of baked beans from the oven.

"You know. The stranger," said Rebekka while carefully spreading frosting on the chocolate layer cake in front of her. She leaned over to make sure frosting covered every spot; that way she didn't have to look up at Mrs. Sampson or Mrs. Knutson. She wondered if they noticed the flush she could feel creeping up her neck.

"Need more eggs for that potato salad?" asked Mrs. Sampson, crossing over to taste the mixture in the bowl.

"No, I don't think so." Mrs. Knutson pushed her friend's fingers away from the food. "And yes to you, Rebekka. I heard him tell Lars that he'll be back."

"Oh."

"Why?" Both women stared at Rebekka as she scraped the bowl for the last bits of frosting.

"I . . . ummm . . . well, it would be a shame to lose a good carpenter like him."

"How do you know that?"

"What?"

"That he's a good carpenter." Mrs. Sampson flashed a grin at her longtime boarder.

"Anyone could see that." Rebekka flipped new curls into the top of the cake.

"Anyone who was watching, that is." The two widows turned to focus totally on Rebekka.

Rebekka wished she had never started this discussion. She kept her gaze on the cake, but her flaming cheeks refused to cool. *One would think you're interested,* she chided herself. *You know better than that. He, whoever he is, is just a drifter, a man passing through. Be grateful he helped on the school and let it go at that.*

She mentally shrugged off the thoughts and, with a grin tugging at the corners of her mouth, asked, "Either of you catch his name?"

The three of them were still laughing as they loaded the wagon to bring the food over to the schoolyard.

They arrived just in time for the church service. Reverend Haugen stood in front of the impromptu altar and raised his hands for silence. People found places to sit on the benches, the remaining stacks of lumber, or the ground. A hush fell, broken only by a bird's song.

"This is the day that the Lord hath made," Reverend Haugen began the service.

"Let us rejoice and be glad in it," the scattered congregation responded.

"Let us pray." The Reverend bowed his head and waited for the rustling to cease. "Lord God, bless us this day as we worship Thee and bless the fruits of our labors. Open our hearts to hear Thy word. Amen." He raised his head and looked over the people gathered. "Today we'll sing the songs we know best since we chose not to bring the hymnals. Let's start with 'Beautiful Savior.'" As his rich baritone rang out the opening notes, everyone joined in.

Rebekka felt the sun warm on her back while a playful breeze tickled the strands of hair that refused to be bound into the coil at her neck. As she sang the familiar words, she let her gaze roam around the gathering. Her pupils, their families, the townsfolk, some who came to church regularly, and some who didn't. She kept her eyebrows from rising when she recognized the saloon owner and exchanged a wink with Mrs. Sampson when they both noticed two of the older youths making calf eyes at each other.

I wish we could worship outside like this every Sunday, Rebekka thought, *at least as long as the weather is nice. Seems to me people feel closer somehow. Maybe it's because we're all working together on something truly important.*

As the Reverend read, Rebekka forced herself to concentrate. "From 1 John, chapter four, 'Beloved, let us love one another: for love is of God...'"

Here, today, her thoughts continued with a mind of their own. *It is easy to love one another.* A black cloud of remembrance dulled her joy. Well, maybe not everyone.

When they raised their voices in the final hymn, she allowed herself a glance around the group again. Now, why was it that the sun seemed to shine brighter when she saw the stranger, leaning against the corner of the schoolhouse?

And why was her neck warm when she caught a grinning Mrs. Sampson watching her?

By the end of the day, the building looked complete—from the outside. A roof, windows glinting in the dying sun, and the door hung above three steps, all there but the bell hanging in the tower.

"Looks pretty good, if I do say so myself." Lars Larson joined her in staring up at the men coming down from nailing the cap along the roof's peak. "Sure is farther along than I thought possible."

"Just goes to show what a determined group of people can do when they set their minds to it. When do you plan to rehang the bell?" Rebekka turned to watch two children playing tag under the ladders. When their mothers called them away, she looked up at Mr. Larson.

"Soons we're done with supper. Thought we'd use that as a good way to finish the day."

"Wonderful."

"Excuse me, Miss Stenesrude, I need to talk to Jude before he gets away," Mr. Larson said as he left her side to stride across the yard to where the man in black, as Rebekka called him in her mind, was leaving the yard.

"At least now I know part of his name," Rebekka said to no one in particular.

"Here, how about pouring coffee?" Mrs. Sampson handed her the heavy pot. "And it's Weinlander."

Rebekka took the pot and scurried off. There it was, that blush that crept up her neck. She'd never flushed so much in her whole life as these last two days. What in the world was wrong with her?

"Weinlander, wait up."

Jude turned at the calling of his name, and he watched as Lars Larson caught up with him.

"You're staying for supper, aren't you? That's the least we can do after all your fine work. I think you're a good part of the reason we got so much done."

"Ja, I'll stay. I was just going over to look at the creek. Pity you had to cut down all the trees along it." Jude tipped his hat back.

"It was that or lose the town. You know, with that fire and all, there's lots of building needs doing before the snow flies. Might you be interested in staying on and working for me?" Mr. Larson caught his suspenders with his thumbs. "I know how good you are. You could run one crew and me another."

Jude lifted his hat and ran his fingers through his hair before using both hands to place his hat back in place. He looked off to the horizon on the other side of town. When he nodded and said, "Guess I could," Mr. Larson let out his breath as if he'd been holding it. "Guess I could."

"You could probably get a room at Mrs. Sampson's boardinghouse. I heard she has a vacancy."

"Well, I better—"

"If it's a case of money, I could give you an advance, and since you're working for me, I know she'll let you pay the rest later. The food's good there, too."

Jude thought of the beans and no coffee he'd subsisted on for the past week. One morning he'd even borrowed a cup of milk from a cow in the barn where he'd slept. When he'd gone to look at the creek, he'd been hoping to see fish. Fried fish had sounded mighty tasty. And how long had it been since he'd slept in a real bed?

He looked back to the waiting man. "All right. But if you don't mind, I'd as soon sleep in your hay barn till it gets colder."

Mr. Larson grabbed his new employee's hand and shook it. "Good. That's Mrs. Sampson over there, the lady with the white hair and white apron who's been overseeing the food serving. Just tell her I sent you." Before Jude could walk off, Mr. Larson put a hand on Jude's arm and dropped his voice, "I'll just pay the room for now."

Jude nodded his thanks. He'd pretty much used up his store of words in the last two days. Everyone had been so nice to him. If they only knew who he really was. The thought caused the two slashes between his eyebrows to deepen. If they only knew, they'd never speak to him again. They'd just run him out of town.

He joined the last of the laborers at the wash bench and, after sluicing down, took a seat on the benches by the laden tables. While some folks had left to attend their evening chores, many more laughed and joked around the tables. Jude listened to the jokes as the two young men beside him flirted with all the young women bringing refills of potato salad, fried chicken, sliced ham, and baked beans down the row.

Mrs. Sampson brought him a piece of apple pie and sat down beside him. "Lars told me you need a room?" She spoke in a low voice, only for his ears. "By the way, I'm Widow Sampson with the boardinghouse."

"Glad to meet you." Jude picked up his fork. "You make this pie?"

She shook her head. "That chocolate cake is my doing. Yesterday I noticed you seem a mite partial to apple pie, so I snagged you a piece before it was all gone."

"Thank you. I'm sure the chocolate cake is good, too," Jude said as he cut off a bite of pie and lifted it to his mouth.

"I have a proposition for you. I need some things done around my place that you could fix if you had a mind to. You could work off some of the board if you'd be so inclined."

Jude turned and looked at the cheery woman beside him. "But you don't know me."

"I know what I see."

Jude wanted to ask her what it was she saw but instead took another bite of pie.

"Well?"

"I'd be so inclined," he nodded. "And thank you."

"It's the big white house off Main Street on Sampson Street."

Jude turned and looked at her. "Sampson Street?"

"Mr. Sampson was well liked by the founding fathers." The twinkle in her eyes invited him to smile back.

Jude scooped up the last bite of pie as he said, "I have a horse."

"I know. I have a fenced pasture behind the house and a shed that could be called a small barn. You can get feed and hay at the Every after you get back on your feet."

Jude swung one leg over the bench so he could face her. "Why are you doing this?"

Without flinching and looking away, Widow Sampson met his gaze and said, "I don't really know. It just seems what I am supposed to do." The two stared at each other, both measuring and weighing the person in front of them. "Is there anything else I should know about you?"

"Not that I can think of," Jude answered without batting an eye. Inside his head he finished, *If you only knew.*

"Then we'll see you back at the house when you've finished here. You can bring your horse tonight or pick him up tomorrow."

Mrs. Sampson rose to her feet. "Stay here. I think I see a piece of chocolate cake with your name on it."

They sure got chummy fast, Rebekka thought as she carefully avoided looking at Jude and Mrs. Sampson. She absolutely refused to let herself amble over to see what was happening.

"All right, folks, let's gather 'round. The pulley is installed for the bell. All you children, Miss Stenesrude, come over here. It'll be your job to pull the rope that will raise the bell." Lars Larson waved his arms to encourage the children to make a line by the rope lying on the ground.

"Miss Stenesrude, you take the end. John, Elizabeth, you bigger kids, start right here." Mr. Larson handed them the heavy rope. "You little ones, line up on both sides. Now, when I count to three, you'll all pull together, understand?"

Children came from every corner, laughing and giggling as they grabbed the rope.

Rebekka looked up on the roof where two men sat on the edge of the tower, ready to secure the bell when it reached its new home. One waved at her.

"We're ready when you are," he called.

"Mith Thtenthrude, can I be by you?" Emily Gordon pleaded with her round blue eyes.

Rebekka stepped back and shared her rope with the little one. "Of course. Now you be ready to pull."

"One," Mr. Larson's voice rang out. Silence fell. "Two." Giggles erupted along the rope line.

"Stop shoving me!" a small boy demanded.

"Get off my foot!" yelled someone else.

"Three! Now, pull steady, don't jerk. You want the bell to rise nice and easy." Mr. Larson walked along with his pulling team as the rope stretched from the tower clear to the ground and along the caterpillar of pullers.

"Good, good!" A man inside of the building who was guiding the bell called. "Easy now."

The line of children snaked back, each one carefully pulling on his section of rope. Rebekka watched as the older ones looked out for the younger and they all worked together to raise the bell.

"There it is!" The cry rang out as the top of the bell cleared the ledge. The two men waved. The line stopped.

"Ith almotht up," the lisper beamed up at Rebekka.

"Sure is. You did a good job." Rebekka leaned down and laid a fingertip on the little one's button nose.

"Don't drop your rope," the charmer cautioned.

Rebekka nodded solemnly. "I won't." She raised her gaze to the bell tower as one of the men called out.

"Easy now. Only an inch at a time."

The children stared up at him, waiting for the signal and then barely moving back. The bell inched upward.

"That's it." The two men secured the bell and raised their hands for the cheer. "Okay now, on three. Pull the rope for the bell to ring. One, two, three!"

The children pulled; the bell rang out, the *bong, bong* sounding joyous and richer for the cleaning. They pulled again and the bell sang for them all.

"Yeth," the little one said, clapping her hands and turning to Rebekka, who lifted the child into her arms. Together they and all the crowd clapped and cheered.

Reverend Haugen walked up the schoolhouse steps and turned to face the gathered people. "A fitting end to a wonderful day. Let us bow our heads and thank the Lord for watching over us." He waited for the rustlings to cease and bowed his head. "Dear Lord, we dedicate this building to Thee. Be with our children who learn here and the teacher that teaches them. We thank Thee for keeping us all safe and in Thy care. Now, please give us safe travel and good rest. Amen."

Rebekka shook hands and wished everyone good night, thanking them for their efforts. As the last wagon was loaded and left, she and Widow Sampson folded tablecloths and picked up the stray napkins.

"What a day," Rebekka said as she rubbed the small of her back with her fists. "Mr. Larson said we would be able to open school next Monday. They'll be finishing the inside of the building this week." She turned to catch a secret smile that Widow Sampson tried to hide. "All right. What's that for?"

"You'll see." The older woman packed the last box into the wagon. "Are you riding with me or walking?" she asked as she climbed up on the seat of the wagon.

"I'm coming," said Rebekka as she stepped up and pulled herself onto the wagon seat. When the horse started off, she looked over her shoulder to the schoolhouse, gleaming faintly in the dusk.

"Thank You, Lord," she whispered.

"What's that?"

"Just happy, that's all."

"That's enough."

"You want me to take the horse back?" Rebekka asked when they pulled to a halt at the boardinghouse.

"That would be nice, dear. Then I can get these things put away. When you get back I have something to tell you." The Widow Sampson stepped to the ground and tied the horse to the fence. Together, the two women unloaded the wagon, carrying baskets and tubs to the back porch.

"I wouldn't mind if you told me now." Rebekka paused before returning to the horse.

"Just hurry back. I hate to see you out after dark."

Rebekka hummed along with the horse's *clip-clop, clip-clop* trot back to the livery. Since no one answered her call, she tied the horse to the hitching post in front and swung off back to the widow's house. As she walked the quiet streets, lights glowed from windows, a dog barked, and another answered. Since it was Sunday night, the saloon was closed and dark.

But there were plenty of lights at Widow Sampson's boardinghouse and Rebekka looked across the yard in surprise. She'd have thought Mrs. Knutson would have gone up to her room and Mrs. Sampson would be finishing up in the kitchen. The gate creaked as she opened it; a horse nickered from somewhere out in the pasture.

Rebekka froze. Who's horse was out there? Had an animal gotten loose and found its way to their pasture? She locked the gate behind her and strode up the walk. Surely she wouldn't have to take a strange animal back tonight.

At the sound of voices, she paused on the back porch. One voice was a man's. Perhaps someone had come for his horse. She breathed a sigh of relief, opened the back door, and crossed through the pantry to the kitchen.

"What?" she said as she saw the stranger, sitting perfectly at ease at the table in Mrs. Sampson's kitchen.

"Rebekka Stenesrude, I'd like you to meet our new boarder, Jude Weinlander." Mrs. Sampson shot Rebekka a look of apology.

"Miss Stenesrude." Jude rose to his feet and tipped his head in the time-honored greeting of male to female.

"Mr. Weinlander." Rebekka knew her manners. What she didn't understand was how one man's eyes could look so . . . so . . . sad wasn't nearly strong enough. Not blank, not dead, just filled with deep-down, soul-searching sorrow. Whatever had happened in his life to bring that darkness to eyes that should have sparkled like the sun, dappling a Minnesota lake in the summer?

Again the slash of silver in his dark blond hair caught her attention. Did he ever smile? What would it take to make a smile light his eyes and crease his face? *Silly,* she chided herself. *He's a drifter: He'll be here and gone before you know it.*

"Mr. Weinlander will be working for Lars," Mrs. Sampson said as she reached for the coffeepot on the stove. "Would you like a cup before you retire?"

Rebekka shook her head. "No, thanks. I think I'll go on up."

The usual camaraderie seemed to have fled the kitchen. Would things ever be the same?

Jude watched her leave the room, her back straight, her head high. He wondered how she could hold her head so straight with that thick braided coil at her neck. It looked heavy enough to tip her all the way over. Tonight she wasn't smiling. In fact, the temperature had dropped ten degrees in the room when they'd been introduced. But he'd seen her smile at the children today. And all the others helping at the school. She had a wonderful, heart-catching smile when she allowed it out to play. Must have something to do with being a schoolmarm.

He picked up the cup of coffee set before him and sipped. No matter. He wouldn't be here long enough to get to know her anyway.

Mrs. Sampson sat down across from him and, with a sigh, stretched her shoulders and leaned back in the chair. "This has certainly been a busy two days. Glad we don't have doings like this too often."

Jude set his cup down and ran a calloused fingertip around the edge of the mug. He could feel a war going on inside him. Why in the world did he have this desire to tell the woman across from him his life's story? Surely if she knew, she would send him packing in an instant. He cleared his throat. He could hear footsteps overhead.

That must be Rebekka's room. Why in the world was he thinking of her as Rebekka? Miss Stenesrude.

He took another swallow of coffee. "I need to tell you some things."

Mrs. Sampson studied him across the top of her cup. "Not if you don't want to, you don't."

Jude pulled at the collar of his shirt. "It's been awhile since I told anyone—in fact, I never have." *Why do you want to do this?* his mind cautioned. What is there about this woman that invites you to tell all? He looked across the table into the most compassionate eyes he'd ever seen.

"You don't need to do this."

"Ja, I guess I do." He took a deep breath and began. "I been a no-good all my life, deviling my older brother and making life miserable for my wife and mother. But I can't make my wife and my mother sad anymore because they are dead and it's all my fault." He continued with his story without a break. "And now you know. So if you want me to leave, I'll understand."

"Do you play an instrument?"

The question surprised him. "What?"

"I asked if you played an instrument."

"I know what you said. I heard you." He stared at the woman across the table. Her smile warmed him clear down to his ankles. He shook his head, feeling a laugh starting down in his middle. "Yes, I play, if you call a mouth organ an instrument."

"Good. That means we'll have nearly an orchestra right here. Miss Stenesrude plays the organ and piano, Mrs. Knutson the fiddle, and I do a fair-to-middlin' job on the gutbucket . . . banjo some, too. I think we'll have some real high times, come winter." She pushed herself to her feet. "More coffee?"

Jude shook his head. "No, thanks." He stared at the woman who had just given him his life back. "Is that all you have to say?"

She poured her coffee and turned to look at him. "No. There'll be no smoking or drinking or playing cards in my house!" Then her eyebrows raised in question.

"Of course not."

"And it's high time you understand that God forgives us when we ask . . . and even before. You need to plug into that. Breakfast is at seven, earlier if you need, I make your dinner bucket, and supper is served at six o'clock sharp. You needn't worry that I'll tell tales on you. Your life is safe with me." She walked over to the sink and set her cup into the dishpan. "I'll show you to your room." She picked up the kerosene lamp and led the way up the stairs.

Rebekka heard them come up the stairs. What on earth had they been talking about all this while? She turned over and thumped her pillow. She missed sitting in the kitchen discussing the day with Widow Sampson. Why had he come along and ruined everything? Now this house that had felt like home felt more like just a place to live.

Chapter 7

Everywhere Rebekka went, Jude was there.

"Howdy, Miss Stenesrude," said Johnny J., her oldest pupil, as he waved at her from his painting ladder when she approached the school on Monday morning. "Sure is looking good, wouldn't you say?"

"I certainly would." Rebekka stopped to admire the sparkling white paint. "You're doing a fine job." She opened the door to find Jude nailing up the thin boards and the chicken wire for the plasterers who were coming next. "Mr. Weinlander," she said as she tipped her head in acknowledgment.

"Miss Stenesrude." Jude continued nailing, the hammer ringing in perfect rhythm.

Now he was here, ruining her joy in the new building. How could anyone else be happy when he stared out at them with such sad eyes? She slanted a peek in his direction. There was no indication he cared whether she was in the room or not; he just continued with his work.

Rebekka paced the room, picturing the blackboards for the wall, where her desk would go, and if she would change the configuration of the children's desks. She'd seen a school building with movable desks, and since the school was also used as the town's meeting hall, theater, and dance hall, movable desks would be a decided advantage.

She took a paper and pencil from her bag and began a list of supplies, including the changes she would like to make. But where could they get the money? She'd have to talk with Mr. Larson to see if there was any left from the bank loan. As she paced, she tapped the pencil end against her teeth.

When finished, she put the things back in her bag and walked toward the door. "Good day, Mr. Weinlander." She kept her voice cool and terribly proper.

"Ummm." The hammering continued without a break.

As she stalked the path homeward, she fumed at the snub. Didn't he even have the grace to be polite?

After having talked with Mr. Larson and called on two families who had recently moved to the area, she walked into the boardinghouse and found him sitting at the table drinking a cup of coffee.

"Supper in half an hour," Mrs. Sampson said as she turned from the pot she was stirring on the stove and smiled at Rebekka. "There's a letter for you on the entry table. And a box arrived. Must be books, it's so heavy. Jonathan brought it over from the train station."

"Wonderful. Thank you." Rebekka crossed through the kitchen and went out without looking that man in the face. Two could play at his game. She stopped at the oak secretary to pick up scissors and knelt by the box. As she cut the strings, she read the address.

"Who are they from?" Mrs. Sampson followed her into the sitting room.

"A school in Fargo." Rebekka folded back the top of the box and peered inside. "Arithmetic, history, reading," she said as she shuffled through the books, setting them outside the box as she dug deeper. "What a gift. This gives me at least something to start with." She opened a letter taped to the inside of the box top.

She read aloud, "Dear Teacher, We are sorry these aren't brand-new, but we planned on sending these to the Indian Reservation after we received new textbooks. Please send them on when you are finished with them. Please accept our sympathy on the burning of your school." Rebekka looked up to Mrs. Sampson. "Isn't that wonderful?"

Jude, who was standing behind Mrs. Sampson, saw Rebekka's shining eyes and felt like a mule had kicked him in the gut. Why, she wasn't plain at all, like he'd first thought. When she smiled like that, her eyes could teach the sun something about shining. And all it took was a box of hand-me-down books for her school, no less.

Jude turned and left the two women talking. He needed to wash before supper anyway. As he pumped a bucket of water at the outside well, he thought back to the school in Soldahl. They had plenty of books. There was even a library in town, at the school, of course. And Mrs. Norgaard had a whole room full of books.

But was he ready to write to them? He sluiced water over his head and shoulders and scrubbed with the bar of homemade soap left on the bench beside the bucket. As he rinsed again, he shook his head. "How can I ask them for something when they've already given me so much? And all I ever did for them was cause trouble."

But this wasn't asking for something for himself, his argument continued. Rebekka's, Miss Stenesrude's—he even caught himself correcting his thoughts—happiness wasn't for herself either. What she needed was books and supplies for her school so she could teach the kids who would be coming to her. Cute kids like the little girl with the lisp . . . and the two young lovebirds.

Jude dried himself with the towel Mrs. Sampson had hung on a nail above the wash bench. He would write the letter tonight. It was for the children of Willowford, after all.

After repacking her box of books, Rebekka sat down in the sitting room to read the letter from her aunt. What a joy it was to have family again. She who had felt alone for so long. She smiled at the news that one of her cousins was getting married, a second was increasing her family, and her grandmother wished Rebekka could come for another visit soon.

Rebekka tucked the letter back into its envelope. Maybe she could go see them for Christmas. What would it be like to spend Christmas with people who were her real family, not only friends, but related? Her mother said they'd had Christmas with her mother and father, back when Rebekka was little, but Rebekka couldn't remember them. Most of her memories were not worth dragging out.

"I'll carry that over to the school for you on Friday," Jude said as he stopped in the arched doorway. "Should be done with the walls by then."

Rebekka started. She hadn't heard him walk across the floor. "Why . . . why, thank you." She looked up in time to catch a fleeting glimpse of something lighten his eyes. No, she'd been mistaken . . . only the dark remained. But she couldn't pull her gaze away. Such deep, dark eyes. All she could call it was sadness.

"Supper's ready," Mrs. Sampson called from the kitchen.

Rebekka let the conversation between the two widows flow around her, answering only when asked a question. She concentrated fully on each bite, but if someone had asked her what she was eating, she couldn't have said. She didn't dare look up for Jude sat right across the round oak table from her, and she knew for certain that if she looked into his eyes again, she would blush enough to light up the room.

"Please pass the bread." His voice, deep and rich like maple syrup flowing over steaming pancakes in the morning, played bass to the women's soprano.

At the sudden silence, Rebekka looked up. "Oh." She passed the bread plate that had been sitting directly in front of her. But she didn't look across the table. No, sirree. She only looked to Mrs. Knutson, who sat on her right and who passed the plate to Jude.

But his hand caught Rebekka's eye . . . tanned, long, blunt fingers. She forced her gaze back to her plate. What was the matter with her?

When she finally escaped to her room, Rebekka gave herself a good talking to. She tried to sit down at the table beside the window to write her letter but instead ended up pacing the floor. *You ninny. You are the schoolteacher, remember? You can't talk to anyone. You have a respected position in this town and that man is only a drifter. Besides that, he doesn't care a bit for you and you don't want him to.*

She kept her shoulders back and her spine straight. When she felt she'd said and heard enough, she sat herself back down in the chair and took out paper and pen and uncapped the inkwell. She dipped the pen and began, "Dear Aunt Sofie . . ."

Her mind floated down the stairs and into the sitting room, where she could hear Mrs. Sampson and Mrs. Knutson and Mr. Weinlander talking. A black blot spread across the white paper. *"Uff da."* Here she was the schoolteacher, who was supposed to teach penmanship, and she'd blotted the paper.

Only women's laughter drifted up the stairway. Did that man have a personal law against laughing?

Rebekka took another sheet of paper from her packet and began to write again but stopped when she heard the stairs creak under a heavier tread.

Then she stared down at the newly spreading black smear and wrinkled the page, dropping it next to its mate in the wastebasket by the table. Now she'd not only not finished the letter, but she had wasted two sheets of paper. And paper costs money.

After asking for paper and a pen, Jude climbed the stairs to his room. He sat down at the table by the window and after uncapping the ink, wrote in a bold, firm hand to his brother, Dag. He pictured his brother reading the letter aloud at the supper table in the big house in Soldahl. They would all be sitting at the long oak table in the dining room—Dag, Clara, Mrs. Norgaard, and Mrs. Hanson, who would be jumping up to serve. Gaslight from the chandelier above the table would bring a brilliance to the room, impossible with kerosene lamps like the one sitting on the edge of the table.

The house was grand, for certain. And his brother had grown into the grandness himself, changing from the shy, filthy blacksmith to one of the leading businessmen of the town, even though he was still the blacksmith. Jude chewed on the end of the pen. Where was the anger and jealousy he'd felt all these years? There was Dag with all the trappings Jude had dreamed of and here he was, a drifter in a town far from anywhere, and he . . . he didn't hate anymore. Had it, too, been burned away?

He finished the letter and addressed the envelope. He'd pick up a stamp and . . . he shook his head. He couldn't even buy a stamp until payday. How could he ask for one more thing from Mrs. Sampson? He put the envelope aside. He'd mail it next week.

As he closed his eyes in bed, his mind flitted back to the sitting room and Rebekka. He gave up. He couldn't call her Miss Stenesrude in his mind any longer. Rebekka, kneeling in front of the box of books. Rebekka, with such joy and delight, he'd almost smiled at her. Almost—until he caught himself.

He turned over and folded the pillow under his head. He'd ask for a stamp in the morning. After all, it was only three days until payday.

By the end of the week, Rebekka had collected two more boxes of books from people in the community. On Friday, while she sorted her papers and books into the desk the doctor in town had loaned the school, she heard a team draw up by the school.

"Hello, Miss Stenesrude," a male voice paged her from outside. Rebekka pushed back her chair and crossed to the window. Jonathan Ingmar, the stationmaster, tied his team to the hitching post planted to the side of the schoolhouse and walked to the rear of his wagon. A flat, wooden crate lay in the wagon bed.

"I'll be right there to help you," Rebekka told him from the open window then dashed out the door and around the corner. But Jude got there first, and the two men were lifting the crate out by the time she arrived.

"That must be the blackboard. I can't believe it got here so quickly." Rebekka walked beside them, ready to lend a hand if the tall, skinny crate leaned too far to the side. The two men carried it to the front of the room and set it on the floor, leaning against the desk.

"I'll get my hammer," Jude said as he strode across the room and out the door.

"I need to get home to my dinner," Mr. Ingmar said. "You need anything else, Miss Stenesrude?"

"No, Mr. Ingmar, and thank you so much for delivering this."

"No trouble. I brought my team in for a shoeing this morning." He cast a glance out the door. "You're sure you're all right with . . . ?"

Rebekka caught his meaning. "Nothing to worry about. Mr. Weinlander and the others are finishing up the school building. Mr. Larson went on home and—" She felt like she was blathering. "So, thank you again." She walked him out to his wagon and waved him off.

When she reentered the school, she heard the screech of nails being pulled. Jude picked up the top section of the crate and put it off to the side as she reached him.

"Brand-new. Can you beat that? I'll be the first person to write on the new blackboard." Rebekka squatted down and ran her fingers over the dusty black surface. When she looked up at Jude, she thought she caught a smile . . . almost. At least his right cheek had pulled back a mite. She was sure it had. She smiled in return—just in case.

"If you give me a hand, we can lift it out right now or wait until the others return."

"Let's do it now. I can't wait to see it on the wall." She paused. "Shouldn't the wall be painted first?"

"We can take it down again. Might not get at the painting until a cold snap anyway."

"All right." Together they lifted the blackboard out and stood it against the wall. "It's heavy."

Jude removed his yellow measuring stick and unfolded it to measure the height and length of the blackboard. Then he measured down from the ceiling and marked on the plastered wall. Lightly tapping with his hammer, he located the studs and drove home the nails needed to hold the heavy blackboard.

Rebekka watched as he accomplished each task with an economy of movement and the sureness that comes with practice and pride in his work. She wanted to offer to help but had no idea how.

"Ready?" He shoved his hammer back into his belt and leaned over to pick up the blackboard. "This'll be heavy."

"I know." Rebekka prepared herself and, with one eye on Jude and the other on the blackboard, hoisted it up and set the back of the frame over the line of nail heads. When it was in place, she gave the oak frame a pat and turned to smile at Jude.

"Thank you. Oh, that's wonderful." With a swirl of her skirts, she spun back and stroked her hand down the frame again.

The smile she gave him lit up the room . . . and his heart. Jude felt like clutching his chest. What could one do with a smile like that but treasure it and keep it safe? Keep it to take out again on a cold winter's night and warm himself when he was far away down the road.

"You're welcome." He forced the words past a lump in his throat. When she turned back, he had his usual expression in place. But he could literally feel his face cracking.

He picked up the pieces of the crate. "If you need anything else, just holler." Crate pieces on his shoulder, he strode out the door.

Rebekka watched him go. Funny, but for a minute there he had seemed almost friendly. She finished up her work and dusted off her hands. Tomorrow the men were slated to build the desks. They'd be crude until later on in the winter, Mr. Larson had told her, when finishing work would be done. Right now he had a house and barn to frame and enclose before the snow fell since both of them had burned in the prairie fire.

Rebekka closed the door and set off for home. She could hear the hammers and saws at work behind her. The men were finishing the privies and the coal shed.

On Monday morning, she arrived at the school early, too excited to eat breakfast. When she opened the door, the fragrance of new wood greeted her and she stopped just to look around. The American flag hung from its stick in one front corner, a globe donated by the mercantile dominated the other. While the children's desks and benches were still unpainted wood, they at least had places at which they could sit and write. Her desk appeared to be the only real piece of furniture in the room.

She left the outside door to the cloakroom open and walked softly to the front of the room. After laying her satchel on the desk, she turned to face the benches. "Please, Father," Rebekka whispered, "bless this year and all of us who come here to learn and to teach. We ask Thy special protection on this place so that all who come here may be safe and feel wanted. Fill me with wisdom and love for all my children. I thank Thee in Jesus' precious name. Amen."

When she opened her eyes she thought she saw a shadow crossing the door. Had someone been there? Immediately she heard two male voices in the schoolyard—Jude's and Mr. Larson's. By the time Rebekka walked to the window and looked out, Mr. Larson was climbing back into his wagon to drive away.

He looked up and caught her wave. "Have a good day, Miss Stenesrude," he called and waved again at her. "Thank you." At his bidding the horse trotted out to the dirt road and turned left, away from town.

Rebekka checked the time on her brooch watch—seven-thirty. Still half an hour until school started. She wandered to the window overlooking the back of the school. Jude stood on a ladder, nailing the shingles onto the roof of the boys' privy; the girls' was already finished. Hat pushed back on his forehead, shirt sleeves rolled back to his elbows, he laid a shingle, nailed it in place, and laid down the other, all with a rhythm born of long practice.

She'd never enjoyed watching a man work before, in fact, she'd never much watched a man do anything. A child's laughter drew her away from the window and back to her desk. The day was truly beginning . . . a whole new year was beginning.

"Miss Stenesrude, see the books I brought." Yes, school had begun.

"That's wonderful." Rebekka walked across the room to stand at the door. Buggies and wagons brought children from the farms farther out; those from town walked across the bridge or ran up the lane. Two tied their horses in the shed.

"John, will you ring the bell?" She checked her watch—five minutes to eight—right on time.

The *bong-bong, bong-bong* rang out across the schoolyard, over the river, and out to town. The children cheered, their voices loud and high with delight. At eight o'clock they were lined up in two lines for the final bell. Rebekka turned and led her charges into their new schoolhouse. Elizabeth led the pledge of allegiance, another child recited a Bible verse, Rebekka led the prayer, and the day was begun.

As Rebekka assigned places at the bench/desks, she collected all the books that the children brought, carefully writing the family's name in each book so they could be returned when finished.

She introduced three new pupils, children of the recent arrivals to the area. All the while concentrating on the children and the beginning of the day, she kept one ear on the hammering coming from outside the building.

"Now I know it will be hard to concentrate with all the noise around us, but I expect you to pay attention just like you always have."

All the children nodded. "Yes, ma'am."

"Now, we all know we are short of supplies, so we will share books. I expect those of you in the fourth grade and above to help with the younger ones."

"Yes, ma'am."

Giggles erupted from a smart comment from the left side of the room, and Rebekka nailed the guilty one with a stern look. "Andrew, would you like to say that so we all can hear?"

A dark-haired boy with faded overalls rose to his feet. "No, ma'am."

"Then we'll hear no more such outbursts?"

"Yes, ma'am. I mean, no, ma'am." He shuffled his feet and looked up at her from under indecently long, dark eyelashes.

Rebekka shook her head and then checked her watch—ten o'clock. "There will be a twenty-minute recess. When you all come back in, I expect you to pay attention. And keep out of the way of the men working."

"Yes, ma'am."

"Excused." The horde leaped to its feet and turned to pound out the door when Rebekka raised her voice. "Order!" The pupils walked sedately to the door, but once through it, broke into shouts of laughter.

Rebekka sank down into her chair. Why did she feel like it should be time for school to be out rather than only morning recess? *It's just the first day,* she reminded herself. *Every year's first day is just like this—except, for the pounding and sawing going on outside.*

As her usual habit, she started reading a book to the entire school the last half hour of the day. "We're going to read one of Mark Twain's lesser-known stories to start this year. It's called *A Connecticut Yankee in King Arthur's Court.* Have any of you read it?" When they all shook their heads, she opened the book and started to read.

Her voice floated over the enraptured children and out the windows to the ears of the man working on a window frame. Jude paused in his measuring. He'd read the story way back when he was in school, but no one with such a musical voice had ever read to him. Schools, they were a'changin', that was for sure.

That night at the supper table, Mrs. Sampson and Mrs. Knutson kept asking questions until Rebekka related her entire day. The only thing she failed to mention was her awareness of a certain carpenter working outside the building.

When she fell into bed that night, she didn't even have to roll over before being sound asleep.

"Was there a rainstorm during the night?" she asked at the breakfast table in the morning.

"Thunder, lightning, the works. You mean you slept right through it all?" Mrs. Sampson set the bowls of oatmeal before each of her boarders.

"I guess so. I'm not sure I even remember crawling into bed." When she glanced for a second time at the empty chair across from her, Mrs. Sampson chimed in.

"Mr. Weinlander ate at six. Said he needed to get a head start on the day, what with so much to do and all. That man, he's a real hard worker, he is."

"Oh," Rebekka said as she sprinkled brown sugar on her cereal and then poured milk over the top. She hadn't really wanted to know where he was, had she?

By Thursday things were settling into a pattern at school. Everyone seemed to ignore the nailing outside and was reading, writing, and working their arithmetic on the no-longer-brand-new blackboard.

After the last child ran out the door that day, she swept the room, washed the blackboard, and settled at her desk to correct some essays she'd assigned during the day. She chuckled as she read one child's highlight of her summer. She'd fallen in a patch of poison ivy on a picnic and spent days soaking in oatmeal baths. "Now I know what poison ivy looks like," she wrote at the end. "And it's not pretty."

Rebekka turned to the next paper and checked the pile of those remaining. She had six or seven papers to go when she heard someone walking up the three stairs to the cloakroom. She raised her head, ready to answer any question one of the workmen would have.

The man paused in the door. Shivers started at her toes and shuddered their way to the top of her head. The last time she'd seen him, he'd been out cold, knocked unconscious by the pitcher she had slammed against his head.

Chapter 8

T hought I'd find you here about now." Adolph's voice wore the sneer she'd heard hissed through the night of months before.

"Will you please leave?" Glacier frost couldn't have been colder.

"Now, don't act thata way. You know we got unfinished business, you and me." He swaggered down the center row, between the benches.

"If you don't leave, I'll—"

"You'll what?" He placed his hands flat on the desktop and leaned toward her.

It was all Rebekka could do to keep from gagging. He'd borrowed his swagger from a bottle down at the saloon, just like that night he attacked her.

"Get out!" She hissed from between clenched teeth. When he leaned closer, she raised her voice, putting all the authority she'd ever learned into the words. "Get out! Don't you ever come near me again!"

Her command ended on a shriek as his hand snaked out and grabbed her by the neck to pull her into a kiss.

Rebekka screamed again and flailed at him with her fists. Suddenly, there was nothing there to hit. Adolph, with Jude's strong hands at neck and seat, was tap-dancing back down the aisle, and then Jude flung him out the door.

Rebekka could hear the thud when he hit the ground.

"And if you ever come near her again, this is only a taste of what you'll get, you hear?" Jude was yelling.

"I'll get you!" Adolph said as he clambered aboard his horse and rode away.

Jude turned and strode back into the schoolroom. Rebekka met him halfway down the aisle, her eyes wild and tears streaking down her cheeks.

When he opened his arms, she threw herself into them. Her braid tumbled down her back and sobs shook her frame.

"Easy now, easy." Jude held her close, murmuring words of comfort, in spite of the hard line of his jaw. By all the saints, he'd felt like killing the young fool. "Did he hurt you?"

Rebekka shook her head and burrowed closer to his shoulder. "I got . . . *hiccup* . . . away last time, too."

"Last time?" Now Jude was sure he'd go after the fool.

When Rebekka finally quit sobbing and calmed down, Jude felt reluctant to let her go. When she pulled back and dug in her sleeve cuff for a handkerchief, he stepped back. "Are you all right now?"

"I . . . I think so." She blew her nose and mopped her eyes.

"Did he hurt you?"

"Do you mean physically or emotionally?"

"Either."

"Or my pride?"

"That, too."

Rebekka took in a deep breath and let it out. "All three."

"That brute!"

"No, no. He just pulled my hair and jerked my neck. He didn't really injure me physically. But why should any man think he can treat a woman that way and get away with it?"

"Did you tell the sheriff last time?"

Rebekka gave him the same look she gave a pupil who'd repeatedly made a dumb statement. Then she studied the knuckle on her right thumb. "I couldn't tell anyone he'd attacked me. He said he'd tell them I en—" she choked on the words, "I enticed him. That I was asking for it. And even if no one believed him, my name would be dragged through the mud and no respecting school system would hire me."

Jude tried to think of an answer to refute her statements but he couldn't. She was right.

"It's the liquor that does it. It's always the liquor." Rebekka shook her head. When she realized her hair was hanging down her back, she reached up to coil it again.

Jude stepped back farther and tightened his jaw. If she only knew. How many times had he teased a woman? How many times had he taken kisses rather than asking? How many times had he been drunk and had no idea the next day of what he'd done?

"I need to finish up outside. Will you wait and let me walk you home? That way we know he won't bother you again."

Rebekka fought a battle with herself, but it never showed on her face. Yes, she wanted to walk home with him. No, she didn't want to come to depend on a man, especially this man who would one of these days be going on down the road. No, she didn't want Adolph to attack her again. Yes, she'd . . .

"I'll be here correcting papers whenever you are ready."

She had to force herself to concentrate on the essays. Whenever she thought of the close call, she started to shake all over. She'd never felt so vulnerable in her own school before. The more she thought about it, the more furious she became. Anger at Adolph, at the liquor, at the men who serve liquor, at those who drink it, smoldered deep within her.

The walk home with Jude passed in silence, both of them caught up in anger at the same situation but from different angles. Jude plotted ways to take care of the young Mr. Strand. Rebekka dreamed of destroying the saloon.

"I'll be ready to leave when you are in the morning." Jude laid a hand on her arm to stop her at the gate to the boardinghouse yard. He continued before she could quit sputtering. "I know you hate having to accept my help but, please, think of the children. If you let me walk you over and back, you'll always be there for them."

"But I . . . I have to go early to start the stove once the cold weather hits."

"I could do that."

"And shovel the steps off and—"

"Some of those things you could ask the older boys to do."

"I do, but they come from so far and have to get home to do their chores. Mr. Weinlander—"

"Jude. I think after what we've been through, you could call me by my given name."

"Jude, then. I really can't ask this of you."

"You aren't. I'm offering." He leaned over to unlatch the gate. "And Miss Stenesrude—"

"Rebekka."

He said her name, as if tasting it on his tongue. "Rebekka, at least try it my way for the next week or so. If Mr. Larson needs me on another job, we'll discuss this. All right?"

Rebekka nodded. "All right. And thank you. I—"

"That's enough. You go on in, I have to wash up."

Rebekka stepped through the gate he held open and walked on up the back steps and into the kitchen.

"Child, what happened to you?" Mrs. Sampson dropped her long-handled spoon and crossed the room to stand in front of Rebekka. Gently, she grasped Rebekka's chin and turned it to the right. "You have bruise marks on your neck. And your hair is down. What happened?"

Rebekka sank down into a chair at the table and poured her story into the widow's sympathetic ear. "I thought Jude was going to kill him there for a minute, but he threw him out the door instead. Thank God he was there or . . . or—" Rebekka closed her eyes against the horror of it.

Mrs. Sampson set a cup of coffee in front of the younger woman. "Here." She dumped two spoonfuls of sugar in it and stirred. "Drink this. You'll feel better."

That evening they all gathered in the sitting room as if in unspoken agreement that no one wanted to be alone. Rebekka sat down at the piano and lifted the keyboard cover. She ran her fingers lightly across the keys, letting the notes seep in to relax the fear and anger from the afternoon. As she drifted into a Chopin sonata, she could feel the tension drain out of her shoulders. Closing her eyes, she let her mind float, feeling the beauty of each measure. Her hands continued to work their magic as she flowed into "Beautiful Savior" and then to "Sweet Hour of Prayer."

Jude watched her from the wing chair in the corner. Lamplight glowed in the auburn highlights of her hair, now slicked back into its tight restriction. Her lashes lay like dark veils on the high rise of her cheeks. The music drew them together, wrapping them in a magic net. But she didn't know that, and he wasn't about to tell her. What would it be like to have a woman like her in his life? He took the idea out and toyed with it, all the while watching the straight back of the woman on the piano stool, swaying in time with the music. But he put it away. He didn't deserve a woman like Rebekka. He didn't deserve any happiness at all. He had killed it long before.

"Why don't you go get your harmonica?" Mrs. Sampson leaned across the intricately carved table between their chairs and whispered so as not to disturb the player. "Mrs. Knutson will get her fiddle and I'll get my banjo. Let's see how we all sound together."

The three left the room at the same time.

Rebekka opened her eyes, finally aware of the near-trance she'd been in. Music did that for her. "Hey, did I play so badly you have to leave?"

"You know better than that." Mrs. Sampson turned at the newel post on the landing. "We're just going to join you. No sense you having all the playing fun."

The two women tuned their strings to the piano while Jude practiced a few trills on the mouth organ. Rebekka spun the stool around, a wide smile replacing the former somberness. "So, what'll we start with?"

"You know 'Turkey in the Straw?'" Mrs. Sampson strummed an opening chord then looked at Jude. When he nodded, she strummed again and away they went. The lively music had all their feet tapping. They played on with each of them calling out tunes.

"That's enough," Mrs. Sampson said, laying her banjo down. "I haven't played for so long, my fingers are near to bleeding."

"Me, too." Mrs. Knutson agreed as she blew on the end of her fingers on her left hand. "These strings are murder. We'll just have to do this more often." She laid her fiddle back into its case. "I haven't had so much fun since . . . since I don't know when."

Rebekka closed the keyboard cover. "You would have thought we've been playing together forever. There won't be a shortage of musicians for the dances this winter."

"How about a cup of coffee? And there's still some of that pie left, Jude, in case you're interested."

Jude stuck his mouth organ into his shirt pocket. "Never could turn down a piece of pie." He stood and stretched his hands above his head. "Lead me to it."

When Rebekka said her prayers that night, she had an extra thank you for the music played in the sitting room. What had started out as a way to let go of the anger from the afternoon turned into a party. "Father, that was such fun. And I think Jude even smiled a time or two. Shame I had my back to them. I'd like to see him laugh sometime. Thank You he was there to . . . to . . ." The anger swelled up unbidden, tasting bitter on her tongue, and she couldn't say the words. She rested her forehead on her clasped hands on the edge of the bed. The hard floor beneath the rug made her knees ache.

"What can I do about Adolph, so he doesn't attack anyone else?" The remembered smell of liquor on his breath made her gag. She waited for more words to come, but she saw only black. "Please help me. In Jesus' name. Amen." She shivered in the breeze lifting the curtains at her window. The bite to it made her think of frost and fall.

She pushed herself to her feet and slipped beneath the covers. This night she was grateful for the quilt to pull over the sheet and blanket.

In the morning, Jude was already gone by the time Rebekka had finished dressing and had entered the kitchen for breakfast.

"He said to wait for him; he'd be back to walk you over." Mrs. Sampson turned the bacon with a long fork. "How many eggs you want this morning? I thought to make you a fried egg sandwich for your dinner."

"Two, I guess," Rebekka answered as she pulled out her chair. "And that sounds fine." She sat down and placed her napkin on her lap. "But he doesn't need to do that. I'll be just fine."

"Don't think it'll do you any good to argue. Seems like when he makes up his mind about something, he don't let nothing get in his way." Mrs. Sampson set Rebekka's plate in front of her along with two pieces of toasted bread. She poured herself a cup of coffee and sat down. "That was some fine playing last night, if I do say so myself."

"You can say that again." Rebekka spread ruby-red choke-cherry jelly on her bread. "Do you think—" She didn't have time to finish her question as the sound of male feet on the back porch cut her off.

"You about ready?" Jude took off his hat as he entered the room.

"You don't have to do this, you know," Rebekka said after swallowing the food in her mouth.

"I know. Finish your breakfast. I'm due for a cup of coffee anyway." He crossed to the cupboard and took out a cup, filled it, and sat down at the table. "Any of that pie left?"

"You know you finished the last piece last night. Will molasses cookies do?"

"Ja, sure." He leaned back in his chair.

Was it just her imagination or had he winked at Mrs. Sampson? Rebekka finished her eggs and wiped her mouth with her napkin. "I'll be right back down."

The walk to the school passed without conversation. Every time Rebekka tried to think of something to say, she thought it sounded silly. Since when did she have trouble thinking of topics to talk about?

"Thank you," she said as she started up the steps.

"Don't leave until I'm ready this afternoon."

Rebekka sucked in a breath, ready to lambaste him for giving her an order, but he was already off around the corner of the building before she could come up with the appropriate words.

The walk home passed without words also. He tipped his hat at the gate and turned back to the school. "Tell Mrs. Sampson I'll be here at six."

Tell her yourself was what Rebekka wanted to say. Instead, she blustered into the kitchen and did as he asked. Guilt at taking up his work time kept her quiet.

But he doesn't have to do that, she argued with herself, her heels tapping out her ire on the stairs to her room. *But you did feel safer, didn't you?* The other side of her argument won.

By the end of the week, Jude and Rebekka had progressed to discussing the day's events on their way home from school. He asked her how the children were doing and, by the time she told him, they were already at the boardinghouse's gate.

"You read real well," he said as he tipped his hat and then strode back to the school.

Rebekka watched him go. Now what had he meant by that? She thought to the open schoolhouse windows. He must have been listening to the story she read at the end of the day. She felt the heat begin at her collar and creep upward. What an unusual man.

On Monday, James Olson returned to school and by Wednesday the other three older boys joined the row in the back of the room. Harvest had finished early due to the extra long hot weather.

On Friday, Jude announced that he was finished with the outside work on the school and would be moving on to the barn Mr. Larson was building for Ed Jameson. They hoped to have both the house and barn usable by the time winter set in.

"I've asked John Johnson to walk with you." Jude tipped his hat and turned away as usual. "He'll be here at seven-thirty Monday morning. He'll also walk you home in the evening."

Rebekka fumed as she strode up the walk. He could at least have asked her instead of telling her. But now that darkness was coming earlier, she knew she'd be grateful for the escort. She could have asked one of the older children herself. *But would you have?* the voice from within asked her. No, she had to admit, she wouldn't have.

Saturday, she saw Adolph Strand at the mercantile and the look he flashed her spelled pure hatred. Rebekka ordered her hands to stop trembling but it did no good. She left without purchasing the writing paper for which she'd come.

That night, the nightmare returned for the first time since the incident at the school. Hands grabbing for her . . . foul breath . . . the smell of liquor gagging her . . . eyes so filled with hate she felt like she'd been stabbed . . . a voice screaming. She sat straight up in bed, her heart pounding enough to jump out of her chest.

The room lay dark around her. Without the friendly moon to light it, all the shadows seemed to hover, strangling her every breath. Rebekka coughed, the sound chasing the shadows back to their corners. She drew in three deep breaths and let them out, feeling her heart slow back down and take up its normal pace again.

She lay down against the pillows and created in her mind the picture of Jesus the shepherd, carrying one of the sheep. "Jesus. Jesus. Jesus." She repeated the name aloud until she could feel the warmth creeping back into her bones. The name faded into whispers and silence as she drifted off to sleep.

When she arrived at the schoolhouse on Monday morning, the new heating stove resided in its place of glory, all shiny black and chrome. After the frost of the last few evenings, the heat would be welcome in the mornings.

"I think we should have a celebration on Saturday night the week after this," she announced at the close of school. "We'll celebrate both the new school building and the end of harvest. What do you think?"

"Will it be a dance?" one of the older girls asked.

"Of course. But I've been thinking. What if we have a box social first to help pay for the new desks?"

As the cheers erupted, Rebekka raised her hands for quiet. "You all make sure to tell your parents, now. I'll post a sign down at the mercantile and tell everyone I see. We'll have a real party."

"When will our desks be finished?" one of the younger children asked.

"Not until after they can't work outside anymore. Maybe we'll have them done for Christmas. I think Mr. Weinlander will be doing them."

"I saw some desks in the Sears catalog. They was real nice."

"Were, Elmer, were nice."

"That's what I said, they's nice."

"All right everyone, let's have a grammar review right now." Groans resounded back to her. "I am, past tense, now."

"I was." The class answered back.

"She or he?"

"Was." One "were" was sounded from over by the window. "They?"

"Were."

"Now do you understand, Elmer?" He nodded. "Let's all repeat it together." The declension echoed from all their throats. Rebekka smiled. "Class dismissed."

At supper that night Rebekka announced her plans. "And I think we could provide some of the music for dancing. This way the same musicians won't have to play all night and not get to dance."

"I'd like that. We need to find another piano player, too," Mrs. Sampson said, passing the bowl of stew around once more.

"We won't have to worry about that. The school piano burned in the fire, remember?" Rebekka dished herself out a small helping. "And I hate to borrow the church organ. Every time we move it, it gets wheezier."

"Organ music just doesn't do for dancing like a piano anyway. We'll do without. There are enough fiddles, guitars, and such," Mrs. Knutson said, setting the bowl down in front of Jude. "Help yourself, young man. You need plenty of fueling for the work you're doing." She patted his arm. "I been hearing mighty good things about you."

Jude looked at her with a raised eyebrow.

"Mrs. Jameson was in today to order a new winter coat since hers burned in the fire. She says the barn's about done and you've started framing the house. This time she'll finally have two more bedrooms. And for their brood, that'll make a big difference."

Jude nodded. "They need more room all right. They've been living in tents since the fire." He helped himself to another of Mrs. Sampson's rolls. "That Jameson has two fine sons. Not afraid of work, let me tell you."

Rebekka listened as the conversation flowed around her. Each night the four of them talked together more, with Jude taking part rather than sitting silently, watching them with those sorrowful eyes. While she hadn't seen him smile yet, at least there was animation in his face. What would his laugh be like? Rich like his voice?

". . . don't you think?" Mrs. Sampson waved her hand in front of Rebekka's face. "Hello, there."

"What? Oh, I guess I was off gathering wool somewhere." Rebekka shook her head. "What did you say?"

Mrs. Sampson grinned a knowing grin. "I asked if you thought we could have this party without any liquor being served?"

Rebekka looked up to find Jude watching her, as if aware her thoughts were of him. She swallowed. She could feel the warmth start below her neck and work its way up. One would think an old-maid schoolmarm like her would be past the blushing stage.

"I certainly hope so." She folded her napkin and slipped it back into its ring by her plate. "In fact, I shall make sure everyone knows that that is the rule." Now she even sounded like an old-maid schoolmarm.

"The men won't like that much." Jude pushed his plate back and leaned his elbows on the table. "And if you want to make money for the school, you want plenty of men there to buy dinner boxes."

"Surely, they can do without for one party." Rebekka leaned her elbows on the table, directly across from him. She could actually feel the steel setting into her jaw.

"Now, now." Mrs. Sampson stood and began clearing the plates. "Anyone for spice cake? I made it this afternoon from a new recipe I got from Isabel down at the post office."

Jude leaned back, breaking eye contact with Rebekka. "Make mine a big piece, please. My mother used to make the best spice cake."

Rebekka felt her jaw drop. The steel melted. This was the first time he had ever mentioned family. She stood and helped Mrs. Sampson clear the table. When she looked a question at her friend, the older woman just nodded.

"Here, you can pass these around." She handed Rebekka the dessert plates. "I'll pour the coffee."

But when Rebekka went to bed that night, she couldn't get over the idea that all men thought there should be booze at every social event, and when it wasn't served, they brought their own. She thought of an article she'd read in a newspaper. Maybe prohibition would be a good idea. The suffragettes were marching both for the end of liquor and the beginning of the women's vote. What would happen in Willowford if the women got together and made their views known?

Friday afternoon the school received its first cleaning by all of the pupils and their teacher. They washed windows, swept and cleaned all the building debris out of the schoolyard, and cleared an area outside for dancing. Since it would be a harvest moon and if it wasn't too cold, the dancing would be outside.

Rebekka lifted her face to the late afternoon sun. Indian summer brought its own kind of warmth—crisp nights, cottonwood and willow leaves turning autumn yellow, the few maples and elms splashed with russet and gold and all the shades in between. But the days called to her, inviting her out to enjoy the last warm slanting rays of sun, yet with a tang that sang of coming cold.

"Mith Thtenthrude." Emily tugged on her skirts. "Look what I brung you." She handed Rebekka three nodding Black-eyed Susans she'd found in the ditch.

"Thank you. I'll put these in water on my desk. They're just right for the party." The little girl smiled, her grin stretching rounded cheeks until her entire face glowed at the compliment. Rebekka squatted down and wrapped Emily in a hug.

Jude saw the two of them, towhead to mahogany head, as he rode his horse back from the Jameson farm. The slanting sun lit the tableau with a golden light, catching him right in his heart.

He pulled on the reins, bringing his mount to a halt, and crossed his arms on the saddle horn. But the moment disappeared as Rebekka rose to her feet and patted the little one on the shoulder. Emily ran off and the teacher looked up to see the rider on the black horse. She waved and turned back to the schoolhouse.

"All right, everyone, I think we're finished. Would you rather leave early or hear another chapter of *Connecticut Yankee?*"

"Read to us. Read to us."

"Everyone find a place to sit, then. I'll get the book and be right back." She turned and entered the schoolhouse, returning in a minute with the book. As she took her place on the top step, children clustered around her like she was a hen with too many chicks.

Jude dismounted and walked his horse into the schoolyard. He folded his legs and sat Indian fashion on the ground, just like the children who turned and welcomed him with smiles as if this were an everyday event.

Rebekka caught her breath. She hadn't expected an adult to join her audience—especially this particular adult. She found her place and began reading. At first her tongue stumbled over the words, but, as she got into the story, she forgot Jude and read to entertain her children.

The night of the party the harvest moon climbed over the edge of the earth and into the sky, huge and golden. While the breeze carried a nip, the warmth of the earth rose to help spread fog veils in the hollows. Laughing people greeted each other as they walked, rode, or drove their wagons and buggies into the schoolyard. When the yard filled, they pulled up along the road.

Rebekka watched as it seemed the entire county turned out for the box social. The tables inside groaned under the fancy boxes, ready to be auctioned off to the highest bidder. Every woman, young and old, had prepared her box in secret, yet hoping a certain someone would buy the right one so they could enjoy the meal together.

She'd brought her box in her bag so no one would see which was hers. Wrapped in blue-and-white checked gingham with a bright red bow, it lay underneath several others. Wouldn't it be something if Jude bought her box? She watched the door, but that certain man hadn't come through it yet.

Lars Larson had volunteered to be the auctioneer for the evening, so when it looked like most of the people had arrived, he stepped to the door to announce the start of the bidding. Everyone crammed into the school building, and even with all the windows and the door wide open, the temperature rose like a thermometer stuck in hot water.

"All right folks, let's start with this little beauty here." He held up a red box with a blue ribbon, ran it past his nose, and declared, "Whoever gets this box will have some good eatin'." He held it high. "Now, what am I bid? Remember folks, this is all for a good cause. Our children need new equipment to go with their new schoolhouse."

The stack of decorated boxes dwindled as the basket of coins filled. Rebekka kept one eye on the table and the other on the door. When Jude finally walked in, she breathed a sigh of relief. When he bid on another box, she felt a stab of . . . She considered the feeling. It couldn't be jealousy, could it? She shook her head.

"Something wrong?" Mrs. Sampson asked from beside her.

"Oh, no, no. I just remembered something."

"Jude arrived."

"I know."

Mrs. Sampson chuckled. Her box went on the block next and Jude bid on it. The price rose all the way to a dollar before he dropped out and Ed Johnson from the mercantile claimed his dinner partner.

Mrs. Sampson fluttered her hand as she left with her partner and the box.

The three remaining boxes looked lonely on the tables that had been so full. Two looked almost the same, both had blue-and-white gingham but one sported a blue bow, the other a red.

Mr. Larson waved his hands over them and picked up Rebekka's. "Now, what am I bid for this lovely creation? I know there are some of you out there without a supper partner. Let's make these last boxes count."

Rebekka kept her eyes straight ahead. She didn't dare look back at the man in the full-sleeved white shirt and dark pants. Without his fedora, his hair gleamed deep gold in the light given off by the myriad of flickering kerosene lamps set around the room. The silver streak caught the light and . . . she refused to look again.

"I'm bid one dollar. Who'll make it one and a quarter?" Mr. Larson continued with the singsong chant of a born auctioneer. "One—there, one and a half."

Rebekka wanted to see who was bidding, but she daren't even look. When she heard two dollars, she swallowed—hard.

Jude's voice rang out, "Two and a half."

Down in her middle, Rebekka felt a little shiver begin. Had someone told him which was her box? She looked to the back where Mrs. Sampson shook her head.

"Three dollars," young Johnson sang out.

"Too rich for my blood." Jude bowed to the younger bidder.

Rebekka felt her heart bounce somewhere down about her toes, but she made sure a smile showed on her face as she stepped forward.

John looked from her to the young woman standing beside her, and Rebekka could see the consternation on his face.

"Why he thought he was bidding on Elizabeth's box." Rebekka looked back to Jude, who shrugged and bid two-fifty on the other gingham box. As he came forward to claim his partner for the supper, he offered Elizabeth his hand. The two young people tried to look happy, but their smiles, even to those who knew them, were forced.

"Well, now," Mr. Larson slammed his hammer down. "It appears to me we had a slight mix-up with the boxes. I thought no one was supposed to know which was which."

"Obviously they didn't," a jocular voice called from the back.

"But fair's fair. You go with the partner who paid for your box."

"Easy for you to say, Jameson," Jude called back. "You peeked."

Laughter floated around the room.

"I have a suggestion," Jude gathered the three of them together. "Why don't we all go outside and eat together? That way we'll all get extra helpings."

The two young people grinned at each other and at Jude. Rebekka's shiver changed to a warm spot. What a thoughtful thing for him to do.

On the other hand, it would have been nice to share a box, just the two of them. *Don't be silly,* she scolded herself. *Put a smile on your face and have a good time.* "Let's go," she said as she picked up one box and handed it to John while Jude lifted the other. "I'm starved. And if we don't hurry, the dancing will start before we're finished."

She followed Jude out the door. Barn lanterns hung from poles around an open area cleared for dancing. She stopped so quickly, Elizabeth ran into the back of her. "A piano," she said, staring at the wagon off to the side. It's load—a piano. "Where did it come from?" She looked from Jude to the wagon and back.

"Well, Nels over at the saloon wanted to give something to the party, so a bunch of men loaded it up and drove it out here," Jude said.

Rebekka stopped like she'd been slugged. "From the saloon? I certainly hope that's all he donated for the night's entertainment."

"Now, Rebekka. Don't look a gift horse in the mouth. You wanted a piano, you got one. Now, come on, let's eat."

Rebekka looked around for John and Elizabeth.

"I thought they'd rather be alone. I remember what it was like to be young and in love," Jude shrugged. "So arrest me, I gave them the right box."

The warm spot in her middle melted and flowed out to her fingers and her toes.

The box could have been packed with sawdust for all the attention Rebekka paid to it. What she really wanted was to make Jude laugh. But, a smile would do.

Jude did a respectable job of demolishing the contents, all the while exchanging remarks with Rebekka about the evening, the people present, and the amount of money earned. What he wanted to say, he couldn't, and a sincere "Thank you" had to suffice. He just wanted her to keep laughing.

The rich contralto joy that flowed through the music of her laugh warmed him clear down to the icy spot that hadn't melted in two years.

He watched a dimple come and go on the right side of her wide mouth. He didn't, no, couldn't deserve her. Slowly, carefully, he drew his cloak of guilt back around him and shut her out.

Rebekka watched him pull back. There would be no smile this night. What had happened to him that . . . ?

"Time for the music to start," Mrs. Sampson announced, appearing out of the circle of light. "You two ready?"

Rebekka nodded. At least this way she could contribute something to the evening herself. And she didn't want to dance anyway. Earlier she'd been looking forward to whirling around the packed-dirt dance floor. But in her dream Jude had been her partner. Something told her for sure that wouldn't happen now.

They played jigs, reels, and hoedowns, sprinkled with waltzes and a square dance or two. They'd just swung into a Virginia reel when a gunshot split the air.

Chapter 9

R ebekka crashed the chords.

"Call the doctor!" The shout came from behind the schoolhouse.

"What's going on? What's happened?" someone screamed.

Pandemonium broke loose with children crying, men shouting, the sound of a fight, fists thudding on flesh. A crash, the sound of a table or some such shattering under the force of a falling body.

Rebekka sprung to her feet and jumped down from the wagon. Lars Larson grabbed her arm. "Get back up there and start playing again. We'll do a square dance, 'Texas Star.' I'll call."

Rebekka, torn between going to see what was happening and listening to the wisdom of Mr. Larson, nodded. She accepted Jude's hand to pull her back up on the wagon bed. After sitting back down on the piano stool, she looked over the heads of the teeming crowd. The doctor with his black bag in hand disappeared behind the building.

"Please God, protect my school. Please don't let them break up what we've worked so hard to replace," she murmured under her breath as she sounded the opening chords. Then, aghast at her concern for the school and not the men involved, she amended her prayer. "And please take care of those who are hurting."

But if they've been drinking . . . She didn't finish the thought, trying instead to think back over the evening. Had men been sneaking out back for a snort or two? She couldn't be sure. She'd been too busy playing and helping all the dancers have a good time.

"We can do this," Mrs. Sampson said over the twang of her banjo. "Jude, you take the melody."

Mr. Larson joined them in the wagon bed. "All right folks, form your squares. Partners ready?"

At their assent, he swung into the call. "Alamen left with your right hand . . ."

Rebekka followed the words, her mind anywhere but on the tune. At least her fingers knew what to do.

"Now, bow to your partner . . ."

What was happening behind the school?

The dance whirled to a close. Applause followed the final chord and Mr. Larson raised his voice again. "Last waltz, folks. Find that special partner for the last waltz." He turned to the musicians. "Choose what you will. I'll go see what's happening and be right back."

Mrs. Sampson took the lead. At her nod, they joined in and played through the tune. After the applause, Mr. Larson again took over.

"That's it and thank you all for coming. Remember to take your lantern or you won't have anything to light your barn with in the morning. Thank you for supporting our school." He waved his arm and the musicians swung into "Good night, ladies, good night, gentlemen . . ."

Rebekka sang along with the others. At the close, she shut the cover over the keyboard and spun the top of the stool around. "Now, Mr. Larson, what happened back there?"

"A couple of young bucks got into it. Nothing serious."

"And the shot fired?"

"Just a flesh wound. Doc took care of it. Now, now, I know what you're thinking. We couldn't search everyone who came tonight. Yes, they brought booze with them. And yes, they'd been drinking."

Rebekka clamped her jaw shut. She could feel the sparks shooting right off her hair she was so furious. If she said anything, it would be too much. Men and their booze. Couldn't they live without it?

Jude watched her burn. The fire flashing from her eyes threatened to scorch anyone and anything in its path. In his other life, he would have been right back there, carousing with the drinkers, making a joke out of anyone who tried to force them to stop.

Now he was on the other side. Now he wanted a life not dependent upon booze to have a good time. He'd been having a great time this evening and he'd felt a part of a group bent on making other people have a good time. But what had it cost to change him?

He hitched the livery team to the wagon and turned around in the schoolyard. "Ladies," he pulled up even with the two widows and Rebekka. "Can I give you a ride home?"

Without looking at him, the three boosted themselves up onto the back of the wagon bed and sat with their feet hanging over the edge. He could barely hear their discussion over the groaning of the wagon wheels under the weight of the piano, but he knew he didn't really want to know what they were saying.

He stopped at the gate to the boardinghouse and let them off. Their "Thanks" came in unison, but no smiles accompanied the word. Instead, they continued their discussion on up the walk and into the house. Jude flicked the reins and the horses walked on. After telling Nels thanks for the loan of the piano, he left the loaded wagon in front of the saloon and trotted the team back to the livery.

While he had a gentle hand on the reins, he kept a tight hand on his thoughts. Too many memories clamored to come forward and be recognized.

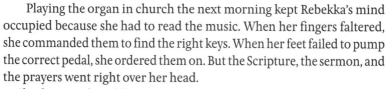

Playing the organ in church the next morning kept Rebekka's mind occupied because she had to read the music. When her fingers faltered, she commanded them to find the right keys. When her feet failed to pump the correct pedal, she ordered them on. But the Scripture, the sermon, and the prayers went right over her head.

She'd seen Jude saddle his horse and ride out first thing this morning. Where was he going? He couldn't be working on Sunday because Mr. Larson felt strongly about honoring the Sabbath. He and his family lined the second pew on the right. Didn't the man believe in going to church? It wasn't like other towns where the pastor had just the one church. Willowford had church only every other Sunday because they were part of a two-point parish. Reverend Haugen lived in St. John, where the other church was located, and he traveled to Willowford.

Right now, she would have liked to travel someplace. Anyplace would do, just away. What were they going to do? She played the closing hymn and continued with a postlude. How could they get the women together? Other than sewing or quilting bees, the women let the men lead. And look where it had gotten them—someone shot in a fight at a fund-raiser and party for the schoolchildren.

She pushed in all the stops on the organ and tucked the sheet music inside the bench. She really needed to practice more if she was to be the church organist, but right now she didn't even want to be that. Why hadn't God taken better care of the evening? After all, she'd asked Him to.

By Monday morning a plan had begun to form in Rebekka's mind.

"You look like the cat that ate the cream," Mrs. Sampson commented when Rebekka sat down at the breakfast table.

"I'll tell you about it when I finish thinking it through," Rebekka promised.

A blustery wind buffeted her and her escort all the way to the school. *At least winter held off until after our party,* she thought as they crossed the bridge. Dry leaves blew before them, the trees denuded by the storm that had sprung up during the night. Rebekka shivered and walked faster.

"We have to get the stove started and the room warmed before the children get here." She looked up to the gray clouds scudding across the sky. "It could even snow."

"My pa says winter's come. He had to break up ice on the stock tank this morning," John said, his nose matching the red of his stocking cap.

Rebekka looked up again. The roof of the schoolhouse caught her attention. Smoke rose from the chimney and blew away on the wind. When they opened the door, warmth flowed outside and invited them in.

Rebekka hung her coat in the cloakroom. "Were you already here?" she asked.

John shook his head. "I bet Jude—ah, Mr. Weinlander, did this."

Rebekka nodded. He'd said he'd take care of the fire in the mornings. A little nettle of guilt stung her mind. And here she'd been downright rude to the man ever since the dance. And all because he was a man. He'd had nothing to do with the fight or the drinking. All he'd done was be male.

She rubbed her hands together over the warmth of the stove. Now she had time to work on her lesson plan. Christmas would be here before they knew it, and what should they do for a pageant this year? But who wanted to have another celebration anyway?

Snowflakes drifted down like lace doilies when Rebekka and John left the schoolhouse that afternoon. Huge, wet flakes clung to their clothes and even their eyelashes.

"You hurry on home," she said as she turned into the street along the boardinghouse. "And thank you for all your help, John. You have no idea how much I appreciate it."

"I don't mind. And thanks for the book." He raised a hand in farewell, his treasured book tucked under his jacket so it wouldn't get wet.

Rebekka nodded. The extra time with John was paying off in more ways than one. He'd become a reader for sure, if she had anything to say about it. And his requesting to borrow a book was certainly a step in the right direction.

She shook the snow off her coat and hat, unwinding the scarf around her neck as she kicked off her boots at the doorsill. After hanging her things up on the back porch, she walked into the kitchen, redolent with the aromas of baking chicken and its dressing. Her stomach growled in anticipation.

"And hello to you, too," Mrs. Sampson said with a laugh at Rebekka's consternation.

"Pardon me." The young woman laughed along with her friend. "Mrs. Knutson home yet?"

"No, and neither is Jude." She peered out the window. "Looks like it's coming down harder."

"Good thing they got the roof on the Jameson house," Rebekka remarked as she went to the sink and washed her hands. When she got the dishes out of the glass-faced cupboard to set the table, they heard boots being kicked against the doorstop on the back porch.

"Well, at least Mrs. Knutson is home safe."

The sparrow-like woman flitted in, still brushing snow from her hair. "Even my hat didn't suffice," she said as she smoothed her hair back up into the pompadour that crowned her head, adding an inch or two more to her meager height. "What a day! Seemed everyone in the county needed something before the snow fell. As if they haven't known it was coming for weeks now." She set her bag of tatting in the dining room. "Three dress orders for Isabel. I think she must be planning a trip or something."

While they discussed the happenings of the day, Rebekka divided her attention between the conversation and the back door where, to her relief, she again heard the thump of boots on the step.

"Good, Jude's here, and supper's ready soon as he gets a chance to wash up. Bet he's near froze after that long ride in. I don't doubt they stay out there during the week if the weather stays bad."

"Sorry I'm late," Jude called as he hung up his things. He stopped at the stove to rub his hands in the rising heat. "Brrrr. When winter comes around here, it doesn't just pretend. This is the real thing. Evenin' everybody."

Heat poured into the room when Mrs. Sampson opened the oven door to remove the roasting pan. Jude leaned over and inhaled the rich aroma of baked chicken. "Now, that alone is worth the cold ride. Gimme five minutes, all right?" He opened the lid on the reservoir and dipped hot water into the pitcher waiting on the counter. Pitcher in hand, he left the kitchen.

"Oh, Rebekka. I almost forgot. There's a letter for you on the hall table," Mrs. Sampson said, brushing back a lock of hair with the back of her hand.

"Thanks," Rebekka said, then went to get it. Compared to the kitchen, the rest of the house felt chilly; perhaps the coal furnace needed stoking. She picked up her letter and ambled back to the warm kitchen. Sitting down at her place, she slashed the envelope with her dinner knife and started reading, mumbling softly. "Dear Rebekka," her aunt wrote in a firm hand. "We are all fine here, but I thought I'd better get our invitation out early. We would love to have you come for Christmas and stay until after the New Year. Grandma especially asked me to invite you."

Rebekka raised her gaze to find Mrs. Sampson watching her. "Is everything all right?" She set the platter of sliced roast chicken on the table.

"They want me to come for Christmas." Rebekka felt a lump form in her throat. She hadn't celebrated a holiday with family in ten years.

"Are you going?" Mrs. Knutson brought the stuffing bowl.

"I don't know."

"Going where?" Jude entered the kitchen in his stockinged feet so no one had heard him coming.

"To Minneapolis . . . for Christmas with my family."

"Sounds wonderful." He pulled out his chair and sat down. "When will you leave?"

But I don't want to leave this family either, Rebekka thought as she looked around the table at the dear faces, these people who were becoming so much more than just friends. This was her family, too. "I don't know." She folded the letter and replaced it into the envelope. *Please ask me to stay here.* She bit her tongue to keep the words from tumbling out. What in the world was she thinking? Of course she wanted to spend Christmas with her relatives, really she did.

But when she went to bed that night, she wondered whom she was trying to convince. Especially since they'd had another musical evening.

She was prepared to wake up to a dark and blustery day, but instead, the rising sun reflected off the crystallized world outside. The elm tree outside the window wore frosting branches and the spirea bushes laid down under their pristine blanket. By the time she and John followed the already-made tracks across the bridge, the sun was glinting off the snow, hurting their eyes. Rebekka looked thoughtfully at a drift off to the side. She hadn't made snow angels for a long time. Perhaps they could do that during recess.

That afternoon, the stationmaster delivered three boxes to the school. "You boys come on and help me," Jonathan Ingmar said as he lugged one box in and set it down by the stove, where everyone was gathered to eat their dinner. Two of the big boys followed him out the door and returned with two more boxes that they set down by the first.

"Who are they from? What are they? Can we open them now?"

The questions flew fast and furious.

Rebekka retrieved her scissors from a desk drawer and handed them to one of the newer children. "Go ahead, cut the twine."

His grin didn't need an interpretation. As he cut the strings binding the boxes, the other children ripped off the wrapping.

"Go ahead." Rebekka answered the question before it could be asked. "The address was for Willowford School. Just save me the return address so we know who we must thank."

As the children peeled back the carton flaps, a letter lay right on top. Emily handed it to her teacher. "Thith ith for you."

Rebekka read the perfect script. It was addressed to Jude Weinlander. She tucked it into her pocket to deliver tonight.

"More books. Look. *Tom Sawyer; Huckleberry Finn.* A whole set of encyclopedias, *McGuffey's Readers* . . . ten of them." The children piled them out on the floor.

"Who sent them, Miss Stenesrude?"

"I don't know," she answered. "But I'll find out."

"Chalk, pencils, paper, even glue." The children sat back in delight. "And colored paper." Down in the bottom of the third box lay three sets of watercolor paints. One of the older girls picked one up reverently.

"I've always wanted to paint," she whispered as she traced a gentle finger over the brightly colored squares.

"And now you shall," Rebekka said, rising to her feet. "Why don't you pack all that back in the boxes for now? As soon as we have shelves, we can put them out."

That evening, when Jude saw the letter, a shutter closed across his face. Rebekka watched it happen. One moment he looked at her with interest, the next he was gone. He stuffed the letter into his shirt pocket and continued with his meal.

Rebekka left it alone until they'd finished supper. When he asked to be excused, she followed him to the base of the stairs. "To whom shall I send the thank you letters? The children are so thrilled with the supplies and would like to thank the sender."

"I'll give you the address in the morning," Jude said then climbed the stairs without another look back. The curve of his shoulders, though, spoke volumes to the woman watching him. She put her hand to her heart; the ache there pulsed for the pain of the man for whom she cared so deeply. Was it the love one has for the wounded or some kind of deeper love? Rebekka wished she knew.

Up in his room, Jude read the entire letter for the third time. While Mrs. Norgaard penned most of it, there were personally written messages from Dag and Clara, pleading for him to come home to Soldahl. They missed him, prayed for him, and were thankful he'd finally written.

Mrs. Norgaard asked if there was anything else the school needed. She volunteered to collect more books and send them on, but Jude would have to let her know.

Jude put the paper down on his desk. She was a sly one, that Mrs. Norgaard. Here she made it impossible for him not to respond. The school needed so much and the thought of a piano flitted through his mind. No, that was a want, not a need. The children sang like larks anyway, with or without a musical instrument to lead them.

He walked to the window and peered out. Much of the snow had already melted. When they finished up out at the Jamesons, he could go home. Mr. Larson hadn't mentioned any other jobs. He listened to the music float up from the sitting room.

"Come home, come home, all who are weary, come ho-o-ome." The words of the age-old hymn, sung in harmony by the three women downstairs, tugged at his heart. Home, where was home anymore?

In the morning he left the address for Rebekka and told Mrs. Sampson he would be gone for a while. They would be staying at the Jamesons to finish up as quickly as possible.

When he mounted his horse in the early dawn and rode down the street, he felt a compulsion to look over his shoulder at the two-storied, slightly Victorian house, smoke rising straight up from the chimney in the still air. If anywhere was home at this time in his life, that was it. Was Rebekka up yet? Was this home because Rebekka lived and played and sang there? He already missed the evenings at the boardinghouse and he wasn't even out of town yet.

The week seemed to drag its feet, like those who plowed through the mud that followed the snow. Early mornings the ground crackled beneath their feet as John and Rebekka broke through the frost cover. But by afternoon, the mud clung to their feet—gumbo they called it. Usually North Dakota soil turned to gumbo only in the spring.

At school one afternoon Rebekka opened the *Old Farmer's Almanac* and read the prediction. This was to be an unusually cold winter, with plenty of snow and blizzards, and an early spring with an excess of rain. *Wonderful,* Rebekka thought. Her pupils would go stir-crazy for sure. Could be this would be a winter when they had to close down during the worst weather. Last year had been mild, so they only missed a week in January.

She rapped on her desk for attention. "Children, finish what you are working on and we'll take time to talk about the Christmas pageant. We'll plan it together, so come up with good ideas."

When she dismissed them that Friday, the pageant's planning was well underway. But she still hadn't answered her letter. Would she go to Minneapolis for Christmas?

Even though the three women didn't overwork themselves, that Saturday equaled three normal ones in the amount of things they had accomplished. Rebekka had just gone to bed when she heard shots ring out. She threw on her wrapper and ran down the stairs.

"Sounds like it's coming from the saloon," Mrs. Sampson said as she opened the front door so they could hear better. Shouts, another gunshot. "That one was the sheriff's shotgun." Mrs. Sampson clutched her wrapper more tightly around her.

The sound of running feet announced the emissary before he arrived at the boardinghouse. "Doc says come quick," he panted. "He needs a nurse."

Mrs. Sampson whirled back into the house to grab her boots and coat. "What happened?" she asked as she shoved her feet into the ice cold rubber.

"Two men down. There was a fight, somethin' awful." He grabbed her arm and hustled her down the walk.

Rebekka closed the door and leaned her forehead against the stained wood. The booze won again.

Chapter 10

M rs. Sampson dragged herself in the door at seven o'clock the next morning.

"What happened?" Rebekka leaped up from the table where she and Mrs. Knutson had gathered for coffee. Neither claimed to have slept a wink. She poured Mrs. Sampson a cup of coffee, while Mrs. Knutson took her friend's coat and hat and hung them up.

With the three of them around the table, Mrs. Sampson took a sip of her coffee and rubbed her tired, red eyes. "It was terrible. One man I didn't know was already dead. Shot through the heart. Two more were injured. One we patched up and sent home. The other, Ole Johnson, Doc worked over all night. But it wasn't enough. He died an hour ago."

"But Ole Johnson has four children at home. Two of them are in my school." Rebekka swallowed the tears that already burned the back of her throat. Those poor babies. What would Ethel, their mother, do now? The family was dirt-poor already.

"I know. We did the best we could. He was shot in the gut. Couldn't stop the bleeding." Mrs. Sampson spoke in the monotone of weariness and despair. "Two men died tonight because two others got in a fight. Ole wasn't fighting. He caught a stray bullet."

"But he was drinking at the saloon when he should have been home with his family. They don't have enough money for food and clothes, but he can spend the night drinking at the saloon." Rebekka felt the fury burn out her tears. "When will they learn?"

"Never," Mrs. Knutson said quietly. "Some men never learn."

Rebekka looked up at her. "You, too?"

The other woman sat straighter in her chair. "My Claude froze one night in a snowbank coming back from the saloon. He said he had a right to have some fun once in awhile, and drinking and playing cards with the men was his idea of the best time."

Rebekka reached across the table and clasped the widow's hand. "For me, it was my father."

"Well, something should be done. More and more I think that closing down the saloons and stills is a good idea. Make booze illegal, that's what." Mrs. Sampson rubbed her upper arms with work-worn hands. "I hate the stuff."

"I hate what it does to people." Rebekka rose to her feet to begin making breakfast. She fetched the frying pan and the eggs from the pantry and the side pork from the safe out on the porch.

"You don't have to do that. Give me a minute to rest and I'll be fine." Mrs. Sampson started to rise, but Mrs. Knutson laid her hands on her friend's shoulders, gently pushing her back in her chair.

"Let us. You've already done your share for today."

"Thank you, both. Thought I'd go out to see Ethel this morning and help with washing the body and readying him for burying." Mrs. Sampson shook her head. "What kind of a Christmas are those poor folks goin' to have now?"

"The funeral will be tomorrow?" Mrs. Knutson sliced the bread and set two slices in the rack over the coals.

"I'm sure, since that's when the reverend will be here. Otherwise he'd have to make another trip." She yawned fit to crack her jaw. "Think I'll take a little lie down before I go."

The three went about the duties of women everywhere who reach out to their sisters in grief. Rebekka fried sausage for scalloped potatoes while Mrs. Knutson baked a cake. When the food was ready, Mrs. Sampson got out a bar of her special soap and several towels. Her box of mercy complete, she walked out to the horse and buggy Rebekka had fetched from the livery.

"We'll take care of things here, don't you worry." Rebekka helped tuck a rug around the widow's knees. "Give her our thoughts and prayers and hug the children for us."

"Will do." Mrs. Sampson flapped the reins and the horse trotted down the street.

The next day after church, the congregation remained for the funeral service. Reverend Haugen said all the proper words but Rebekka had a difficult time sitting still and listening. During the prayers she gripped the back of the pew in front of her to keep from leaping to her feet. This man's death wasn't God's will. If he'd stayed home where he belonged he'd still be singing with the rest of them, rather than leaving his wife to weep and his children to sob for their father. She bit her tongue to keep from shouting the words aloud.

"Dust to dust," the reverend intoned the words at the cemetery. But after Ethel Johnson and her oldest son each tossed a handful of dirt on the pine box, she straightened her shoulders and turned to the other mourners.

"Please, do something about this evil in our town. Good men can't be safe when the booze takes over. Do something before other tragedies happen." She wiped her eyes. "Please. Do something."

Rebekka clamped her hands together. The idea that planted itself in her mind after the fight at the box social had matured. Like wheat nodding in the field, the plan was ready for harvest.

"Tell every woman in town that we will be meeting at the church tonight at six o'clock. If we hurry, we can catch some of the farm wives also."

Quickly, the word spread. When anyone asked a question, the answer rang the same—just be there.

That night Rebekka stood at the front of the pews watching as the women filed in. She closed the doors when it looked like every woman in town and the surrounding area had arrived. After taking her place again at the front of the room, she raised her hands for silence.

"I know you are all wondering why we called this meeting, but after the sad afternoon and Ethel's, Mrs. Johnson's, plea, I think you can guess what we are about."

Gaining courage from all the nods and assents, Rebekka continued. "Many of us have suffered because our men drink. If I polled the room, I'm sure you all have stories to tell. My father was the drinker that ruined my young life. My mother died, I think, of a broken heart. He died because his body couldn't handle any more liquor." She continued with her story and finished with, "I never told anyone this before because I was too ashamed. I thought other people would look down on me because my father had been the town drunk, one of them anyway. And wherever we went." Rebekka looked out over the heads of the women gathered. "Now is the time to do something about this problem in Willowford."

Silence lasted but for a moment when a woman in the back rose to her feet and started clapping. Others joined her, and soon all of the women were on their feet, clapping. The applause soon became as one pair of hands, the steady beat from the heart of each woman.

Rebekka nodded and smiled. When she raised her hands again, the women fell still. "I have a plan. You want to hear it?"

The answer came as one voice. "Yes!" The women took their seats.

"We start with the legal process by talking with Sheriff Jordan. We'll ask him to close the saloon."

"He won't do nothin'. He's a man." The comment came from the back of the room; laughter greeted the sally.

Rebekka went on to outline steps two, three, and four of her plan. The women applauded again. "Now remember, this plan is our secret. The good Lord sees in secret, but the men won't."

"Unless someone blabs," a woman off to the right called out.

Mrs. Sampson rose to her feet, stretched herself as tall as she could, and ordered, "No one will blab." She stared around the room, daring someone to argue.

Nobody said a word.

"Now, who will call on the sheriff with me?" Rebekka asked after the silence stretched to give anyone a chance to comment.

Three hands went up. Mrs. Johnson from the mercantile, Mrs. Sampson, and, Rebekka caught her breath in surprise, Mrs. Larson.

"Good. We will let you all know what happens. And if that fails—"

"Like we know it will," another voice interrupted.

"We'll see you all on Friday night. You know where." The women stood as one and filed out into the night.

The next afternoon after school, the four women met at the boardinghouse. "Ready?" Mrs. Sampson looked at each of them directly. For a change Mrs. Larson didn't have much to say.

"Who wants to do the talking?" Rebekka asked.

"Let me start." Mrs. Sampson pulled her red knitted hat down over her ears. "I have plenty I want to say to him—and all the men."

As they entered the sheriff's office, Sheriff Jordan pushed his chair back and rose to his feet. "Well, hello, ladies." Steam rose from the coffee cup at his left. "What can I do for you?"

Rebekka clamped her lips together at the syrup dripping from his voice. He surely wouldn't be so sweet when they finished with him.

The women took up their places as if assigned. One on each side of the desk and Mrs. Sampson in front.

"Sorry I don't have enough chairs to go around. I wasn't expecting company," he said, his smile faltering slightly at the corners.

"We want to talk about the shooting on Saturday night."

"Now you know I can't discuss a case like that. I have the two men in lockup who accidentally did the shooting. Or rather who are accused of the crime."

"And when their lawyers post bail, they'll be out on the road again." Mrs. Sampson leaned her arms on the desk.

"Well, ja. That's the way our legal system works. Everyone is innocent until proved guilty. We'll have a trial and—"

"And the most they'll get is manslaughter because, after all, it was only a fight and no one meant to do any harm."

"Well, now, Alma—"

"Mrs. Sampson."

He looked at her for a moment and tightened his jaw. "Mrs. Sampson, that's for the judge and jury to decide."

"A jury of all men."

"Now you know the laws, Al . . . Mrs. Sampson." The sheriff leaned on his straight arms, towering above the woman across the desk. "Now, what can I do for you ladies?" He cut the end of each word like a sharp cleaver through chicken bones.

"You can close down the saloon so there won't be any more such 'accidents.'"

"Now you know I can't do that. The Willowford Saloon is a reputable business. Nels pays his taxes just like everyone else. Why, he even loaned out his piano for the school party . . . out of the goodness of his heart. You know that, Miss Stenesrude." He shook his head. "What you're asking, I just can't do that."

"In spite of all the fightings and killings caused by the liquor served there?"

"Now, that was an accident, I told you—"

"That leaves us no alternative but to deal with this ourselves. Good day, Sheriff. Ladies?" Mrs. Sampson turned and strode out the door, the three other women following like soldiers behind their general.

Evenings, the three women at the boardinghouse plotted and planned. During the day, other women were seen coming and going. While all their errands looked legitimate, the boardinghouse hadn't seen such activity in years.

It's a good thing Jude isn't here, Rebekka thought one night as she finished her prayers and crawled between the icy cold sheets. *He'd have tried to stop us for sure.* But oh, when she thought of it, how she missed him. They hadn't had a musical night since he had left.

Friday night at eight o'clock the women gathered at the church. Whispers sounded loud in the dark, as they huddled together both to keep warm and to receive their instructions one last time. Axes, hatchets, and a buggy whip or two were drawn from satchels and from under coats.

"Now, remember," Rebekka spoke in a low, but carrying voice. "Be careful you don't hurt yourself and do not do the men harm. Just the saloon."

"All right. May God be with us." She raised her voice in the old marching hymn. "Onward Christian soldiers, marching as to war ..." Fifty women, young and old, marched out of the dark church and formed a line, four abreast, to sing their way down the street.

They sang their way the three blocks to the saloon, up the wide wooden stairs with their feet in perfect rhythm, stomped across the wooden porch and through the double doors, now closed against the winter's cold.

They sang as they laid the whips about, driving the men from their gaming tables like cattle in a drive. They sang while they smashed all the bottles lining the glass shelves behind the bar and chased the few diehards with their axes. The third verse swelled while they made kindling of the tables and chairs. "Forward into battle ..." The words sung from fifty throats could be heard above the crashing, the smashing, and the yelps as men ran out the door.

The shotgun roared as Sheriff Jordan slammed the doors open.

Rebekka and her platoon of ten lined up behind the carved walnut bar with a marble top and, on "Three," they all shoved, tipping the entire bar over on its side. The front was already splintered by the swinging axes.

"That's enough!" Sheriff Jordan roared, loud as his gun.

"Onward Christian soldiers, marching as to war ..." The women swung into the chorus and, shouldering their axes, marched out the door.

"Just keep on marching right to the jail," the sheriff boomed his order. He stood to the side as the marchers left, eyes straight ahead like good soldiers. "Oh, no. Ann, Mary, what are you doing here?" His wife and seventeen-year-old daughter faced forward and marched with their sisters.

The singing women turned right into the jail and marched in. Those who couldn't force their way through the door marched in place and sang in time on the porch and in the street. Their marching and singing kept them warm, in spite of the night wind that growled across the plains, promising snow and cold to freeze one's bones.

"Let me through. Excuse me. Sheriff!" Nels pushed his way into the packed jail. When he finally made it to the sheriff's desk, he leaned on his arms, panting and glaring like a mean hound who'd just been whupped.

"I ... want ... to file charges. These women destroyed—" His voice rose to a shriek. He took a deep breath and started again in a lower key. "These women destroyed my saloon. The only thing left in one piece is the piano." His voice rose again. He heaved and puffed, trying to get his breath again.

"I know, Nels. I was there, remember?" Sheriff Jordan stood at his desk.

"Well, you didn't come quick enough. They broke everything—"

"I know, except the piano." The sheriff raised his voice to be heard over the singing. "Cut it out. Quiet!"

The women sang on, their faces forward, looking neither to the right nor the left.

"Alma!"

"Mrs. Sampson." Her voice cut through the air like the buggy whip she'd used earlier.

"I want to press charges." Nels thumped his fist on the table. "Put them all behind bars. Look what they did to my saloon." He thumped again.

Sheriff Jordan swung around, his fists clenched. "Just get outside right now, Nels, before I throw you in the clink. I got fifty women here to deal with and I ain't got enough jail cells for ten. You got any better suggestions, you just tell me now or leave. I'll talk with you later."

"Well, I never!" The saloon owner looked around the room until he was impaled on Mrs. Sampson's glare. "I'll be back." He pushed his way out of the room, no "Please" or "Excuse me" left in his gullet.

Mrs. Sampson and Sheriff Jordan faced each other over the desk again, like a replay of the Monday before.

The women kept on singing.

Out of the corner of her eye, Rebekka watched the standoff, careful to keep on singing even though her throat felt raw like a ground-up piece of meat. She tried to keep a grin from cracking her face. The orders had been to keep a straight face and keep on singing. She tried to hear what they said but, short of moving out of her place, she couldn't distinguish the words.

Their faces said plenty however. Glare for glare they stared and stormed like two bears over a kill.

Sheriff Jordan threw his arms up in the air. "All right, ladies, about face. Go on home. And stay there!" His roar matched the shotgun that he used for crowd control.

The singing stopped.

"And what are you going to do about the saloon?" Mrs. Sampson cut through the silence.

"I don't know."

The women turned as one and marched out the door. Out on the street, they let themselves smile for the first time.

Rebekka watched them head for their homes. *But what will they face when they get there?* The thought wiped the smile from her face.

"Don't you worry none about us," Mrs. Jordan said in a low voice, as if having read Rebecca's thoughts. "We know how to handle these men of ours, most of us anyway."

Chapter 11

"Nels won't be rebuilding."

"What? You mean that?" Rebekka asked as she dropped her satchel on the table. "How did you hear?"

"Sheriff Jordan came by to say there are no charges being filed. Gave me a lecture on civil disobedience, however." Mrs. Sampson spread the frosting on a chocolate layer cake in front of her. "Said if he'd had a bigger force, he'd a'clapped us all in jail until we rotted." She turned the cake, her eyes twinkling above the smile that came and went. "But he'da needed a bigger hoosegow, too."

"But what will Nels do about the saloon?" asked Rebekka as she dipped a finger in the bowl and licked off the frosting.

"Well, the building wasn't his, he rents it, so I 'spect he'll build a place somewhere on the outside of town." She checked the cake to make sure she hadn't missed any spots.

"Then we failed." Rebekka felt her shoulders slump.

"No. We stood up for what we believed and now the men of this county know their women can accomplish something when they all get together. But unless prohibition goes through, there'll always be places men can drink and play cards. You gotta remember, some women like to join them."

In mid-November, the setting sun was slanting across the snowdrifts when Jude was returning to the boardinghouse. As he rode past the school, he wished it were earlier so he could have given Rebekka a ride home or at least walked with her. The snow in the schoolyard had been trampled by many feet, a circle for "Run, Goose, Run" packed by the game players.

Just past the school he saw three angels formed in the snow, one large and two small. "Who do you think made those?" he asked the only live creature around, his horse. The black gelding tossed his head and snorted. Jude shook his head. Here he was, the man who'd rather not talk with anyone and now he was so starved for conversation, he even talked with a horse.

"It's all her fault, you know." Prince nodded then tugged on the bit. Home lay just across the wooden bridge. "What am I to do?" Prince lifted his tired feet a bit higher. He pulled at the bit again, his ears pricked toward the town ahead.

The horse's feet thudded across the bridge. Beneath, the creek lay frozen, drifted snow filling the creek bed nearly to the tops of the banks. Snow muffled the clop, clop of the hooves on the timbers.

The stillness of the schoolyard and winter silence of the creek made the jangle of the bit ring loud on the crisp air. Somewhere ahead a door slammed. Smoke curled up from chimneys and lighted windows beckoned a traveler home.

Prince turned on Sampson Street and broke into a trot. "I have to tell her, don't I?" Prince shook his head and picked up the pace.

Before he headed up the walk to the house, Jude led the horse into the barn, threw in some hay, and dumped a pan of oats in the manger. By the time he hit the back porch, he was nearly running. He leaped up the steps and kicked snow off his boots. His coat caught the hook along with his hat, and his saddlebags hit the floor. He pulled off his boots at the jack and padded to the door to the kitchen. Heavenly smells assailed his nostrils, and the sounds from inside said supper wasn't yet on the table.

As he opened the door, he knew why he was so excited—he was home! Rebekka jumped up from grading her papers at the table and took a step toward him, her smile wide as the sun on a summer day.

"Welcome home, stranger." Mrs. Sampson spun around and gave him a hug.

Jude stopped as if he'd been struck.

Mrs. Sampson patted his cheeks with both her hands. "Does you good, boy. You need more affection in your life. Just want you to know how much we've missed you." He looked over her shoulder to Rebekka.

What he wouldn't give to have her in his arms instead. He returned the older woman's hug and squeezed Mrs. Knutson's hand. When he straightened, his gaze refused to leave Rebekka's. The two looked deep into the other's eyes, all the while separated by five feet of kitchen floor and a lifetime of sorrows and fears, hopes and dreams.

"Hello, Rebekka," his voice cracked.

"I . . . we're glad you're back." She clamped her fingers around the back of the chair so she wouldn't throw herself in his arms. Why could Mrs. Sampson hug him? What would happen if she just walked across the canyon separating them and into his arms? What would he do? What would she do?

"I hear you're a prohibition rabble-rouser."

"Oh." She mentally shook herself. A grin broke loose and shattered her reserve. "It was nothing. We just busted up a saloon and almost got thrown into prison. All fifty of us, all women."

"Way I heard it, there were axes flying and whips and over a hundred yelling and screaming womenfolk, driving the poor men of Willowford right out into the cold of night."

Rebekka threw back her head and laughed, a contagious sound that invited everyone to join in. "So that's how the story has grown." She looked to the two widows who were chuckling along with her. But when her gaze returned to Jude, her breath stopped.

He was smiling. A real smile that banished the sadness from his eyes and crinkled the corners. "You women are some piece of work." Even his teeth showed.

It was all she could do not to fling herself across the space. He smiled! Jude, the sad, not only spoke a longer piece than she'd heard from him yet, but his smile . . .

"Supper's on the table soons you wash up." Mrs. Sampson plunked a pitcher of hot water in front of Jude. "Your room's been closed up, so it'll be a mite chilly, but leave the door and the register open and it'll be warm in no time."

"Thanks." Jude walked back out into the back entry, picked up his saddlebags and then the pitcher on his way back through the kitchen. "You musta known I was coming." He nodded at the cake on the counter.

"If I'da knowed you was coming, I'da baked you an apple pie." Mrs. Sampson turned to finish the gravy she was stirring on the stove.

Rebekka heard a ghost of a chuckle float back from the dining room. A smile and a chuckle all on the same day? Would wonders never cease?

That night after filling Jude in on all that had gone on in his absence, they broke out the instruments and played all the tunes they could think of.

"How 'bout another piece of cake with our coffee?" Mrs. Sampson asked as she put away her gutbucket. "This sure has been mighty pleasurable."

Rebekka closed the cover on the keyboard. "I'd love some." She spun around on the stool and caught herself falling into the deepest blue eyes she'd ever seen. Clear, warm, like a lake on a summer's day.

"Me, too." Jude reached for her hand and pulled her to her feet. "Rebekka, we need to talk."

"Cake's on." Mrs. Knutson stopped in the doorway arch. "Oh, excuse me ... I mean ..."

"We're coming." The mood lay in tatters at their feet.

As Christmas drew nearer, the days seemed to move in double time. Rebekka, like many others, ordered many of her Christmas gifts from the Sears catalog, at least those she didn't make herself. As the packages arrived on the train, she wrapped them and placed those for her family in a trunk. She'd take them with her when she boarded the train for Minneapolis the day after the pageant.

At school, preparations for the pageant progressed on schedule. One night Rebekka asked Jude if he would help make the sets for the Christmas play.

"Of course. When would you like the help?"

"Would tomorrow be all right? John and two of the other boys need some carpentering help and then the painters can go to work."

"Sounds like a major production."

"Oh, it is, and the children wrote most of it themselves. They even composed two songs to use." She sat down at the piano and played through both tunes, singing the words along with the melody. "See, aren't they wonderful?"

Jude nodded. *Yes, you are,* he thought. *Wonderful and beautiful and ...* He closed his thoughts off like shutting the damper on a stove. And not for him. When he told her what he'd done, she'd close down that wonderful smile and turn away, afraid to be with a man who had killed his wife.

The day before the pageant, the blizzard struck. It howled across the plains and the Missouri for three days, burying everything in drifts ten feet tall and twice as wide. Then it shoveled up the drifts and tossed them in the air, blowing with a fury unstopped by humans or their flimsy houses.

No one ventured out. The trains stopped in the nearest town. Only the furious wind, driving the snow before it, lived on the prairie.

On Christmas day, the world awoke to silence. Silence so deep it hurt the ears to hear it. While bitter cold captured the drifted snow and froze it into mountains and ridges, the sun reflected off the glittering expanses to blind anyone who ventured forth.

"Are you sorry you couldn't visit your grandmother?" Jude asked as he and Rebekka stood at the kitchen window. They could see the rope connecting house and barn that lay partially buried beneath the frozen crust. Jude had followed it to go out and feed Prince during the storm.

"I'm more sorry about the pageant. The children worked so hard and, for some of them, the presents at school might have been the only ones they received."

"You can always put it on in January."

"We will. It's just that they were so excited. You lose some of that with delaying," Rebekka sighed and turned from the window. She couldn't tell him she'd been glad to see the blizzard that stopped the trains. She wouldn't want to be guilty of wishing anything as awful as that storm on the farmers and townsfolk alike, let alone all of God's other creatures.

After dinner, they gathered in the sitting room around the piano to sing all the carols they knew and then some over again. Mrs. Knutson brought out her Bible and read the Christmas story from the Gospel of Luke.

Rebekka heard herself saying the so-familiar words along with the reader. "And in those days . . ." Into the hush of the afternoon, the story carried the same message as it has all through the ages. A Babe was born, the shepherds and angels rejoiced. When Mrs. Knutson closed her Bible, they all sat in silence for a time.

"I love the part where 'Mary kept all these things, and pondered them in her heart.'" Rebekka leaned her head against the high back of the wing chair.

"I wonder about the innkeeper. Here I have a boardinghouse. What would I have done if I was full up and a young couple came, asking for a room?" Mrs. Sampson rubbed under one eye. "It's so easy to sit here and say 'Shame,' but what would I have done?"

"Knowing you, you'd have moved them right into the sitting room and helped deliver the baby yourself," Mrs. Knutson said, smiling at her dear friend. "You've never been able to turn anyone away."

"Thank you. I always said God gave me this big house for a reason."

Jude listened to the exchange, agreeing wholeheartedly. She could have turned him away but she didn't. "I think about the shepherds who believed what the angels said and right away went looking for the Baby. Shepherds are a mighty tough audience. But then, I guess if the whole sky starts singing and you see a multitude of angels, that oughta about you convince anyone."

What about you? Rebekka thought, trying to listen to what he was saying between the lines. *Will it take the entire heavenly choir to convince you that God loves you no matter what?* Love, what a wonderful word. She turned it around in her mind, looking at it from all angles. She loved her teaching and her students, playing the piano, singing. She loved the sun on her face and the breeze in her hair. She loved Jude. Wait a minute! Sure, she loved Jude like a friend and brother in Christ.

But Mr. Larson was a brother in that way also and walking with him didn't set her toes to tingling. Her toes and all other parts inside and out. Sheriff Jordan's smile didn't make her go mushy in her middle.

She used the conversation flowing around her to watch the man who set her heart afire. While he rarely smiled, she knew what it did for his face now. And his voice, that deep, melodic way he had of talking, as if he thought out each word in advance so as to use the best one. She hadn't planned to feel this way about any man. Was this her Christmas gift from the Lord of Hosts?

"I have something for each of you." Mrs. Sampson rose to her feet. "It's not much but, well, what would Christmas be without presents?"

Each of them went to their rooms and returned with wrapped gifts. Rebekka handed hers around and sat back in the wing chair to open her presents. A lace collar made by Mrs. Knutson, a warm muffler with matching hat and mittens in a warm rust color that set the roses blooming in her cheeks from Mrs. Sampson, and the third box, she hesitated to open. She looked up to catch Jude watching her, the smile lurking at the corners of his mouth.

She unwrapped the parcel. Inside knelt a hand-carved wooden angel, her arms spread as if to welcome the world. The feathers on her wings, carved in intricate detail, invited the caress of a fingertip.

Rebekka struggled against the tears clogging her throat and burning her eyes. "She's . . . she's just beautiful." She looked up to see Jude watching her. Was that love she saw glowing in his eyes? Could she feel the way she did and not have him return the feelings?

"My, my, son, I didn't know you could carve like that." Mrs. Sampson shook her head. "You're a real artist."

"I didn't know, either. Out there at the Jamesons, old Grandpa spent his evenings whittlin' so I asked him to show me. That little angel was hiding in a hunk of cherry wood, just waiting to come out."

"Thank you. I've never had such a perfect present." Rebekka traced the grain of the draped gown. "She's so beautiful."

Like you, Jude thought but didn't say. He had no right to say such things, but he couldn't stop thinking them.

Mrs. Sampson opened a set of eight napkin rings of rich walnut and Mrs. Knutson two spools for her lacemaking.

Jude opened his presents as if he couldn't believe anyone would give him something. The red muffler from Mrs. Knutson he wrapped around his neck, the gray wool socks from Mrs. Sampson he promised to wear the next day, and the final package he held in his lap. His fingers had a life of their own as they untied the silvery bow and carefully pulled apart the paper. The mouth organ lay in a bed of tissue, gleaming as the light hit the chrome-and-brass trim. He picked it out of the nest and put it to his mouth. Long, sweet notes hung on the air, each a part of another, as he played "Silent Night."

Rebekka could feel the shepherds quaking and the glories streaming down. The room, her heart, seemed full of the glories of Christmas.

"Thank you." His words blended with the notes hanging in the room as if loathe to part. Other words hung on the air between the two young people, unspoken words but feelings deep enough to withstand the not telling.

After the new year, Rebekka started reading *The Pilgrim's Progress*, since the storms continued unabated and everyone was virtually housebound. One night they remained in the sitting room after the reading when Mrs. Sampson asked what they thought the story meant.

"Nothing," Jude said, looking up from his carving. "It's just a fine story, that's all."

"No, it's an allegory." Rebekka kept her finger in the place. "And all allegories have a meaning." Jude just shook his head.

"This is the story of all of us who fail and fall," Mrs. Sampson said with certainty. "It shows how God always comes to meet us. He picks up his fallen children, dusts us off, and sets us on the right path again. We can never be so bad that He gives up on us." Jude snorted, the shake of his head nearly negligible.

"It's true." Mrs. Knutson joined the discussion. "All we have to do is ask for forgiveness and He gives it. That's why Jesus died, for our sins."

"Well, it's a good story." Jude held the piece of wood he worked with up to the light. "A real fine story."

"Remember that God even forgave Paul after he helped kill Christians, made him into a real leader in the church and for all of us." Mrs. Sampson laid her knitting in her lap. "I'm just grateful that He did it, that's all, or I wouldn't be here."

Jude looked up at her in surprise. Surely a woman such as she had done nothing serious enough to think about leaving life?

But when he climbed the stairs that night, he couldn't shake the thought. Would God really forgive all that he'd done wrong?

Chapter 12

School resumed in mid-February. Rebekka stood before her pupils. "Welcome back and let's pray that's the last of the bad weather."

"When ith the pageant?" Emily raised her hand from the front row. Her feet could now touch the floor as she sat so straight in her new desk.

"How about the first of March? That will give us two weeks to prepare." The children cheered and fell to their lessons with a vengeance so they could have time to practice.

The pageant went off without a hitch. The curtain pulled back when it was supposed to, no one forgot their parts, and, at the end, the audience cheered for five minutes. But Jude's smile was the best accolade Rebekka could have wished for.

One morning Rebekka awoke to the music of dripping icicles. The chinook blew in during the night and was turning the snow to mush as rapidly as it could. The snow seemed to disappear almost overnight.

But when the rains came in torrents, the town began to worry. The Missouri was still frozen, there hadn't been time for the ice to melt, and now, with all the rain, there could be trouble.

Rebekka grumbled on her way to school one morning. First the prairie fire, then the blizzards and the terrible cold, now rains that seemed to be reenacting the forty days and forty nights of Genesis.

Bryde Creek rushed under the bridge but just barely. Another six inches and the bridge to the school would be impassable.

How was she supposed to prepare her students for the examinations when they hadn't been in school for half of the year?

Saturday, a watery sun peeped through the clouds. Sunday, Jude rode Prince out over the prairie rather than take up Rebekka's invitation to join them in church. When he rode past the church, he heard the congregation singing; he pulled Prince to a halt.

"Throw out the lifeline, throw out the lifeline, someone is drifting awa-a-y . . ." The words poured out of the cracks and crevices of the country church as if sung for his ears alone. He nudged his mount into a trot. Maybe next time the pastor was in town, he'd go with Rebekka. Couldn't hurt.

Monday, the rains returned, drenching the land and running off the ground still frozen under the mud.

Some of her students had stayed home and, by one o'clock, Rebekka toyed with the idea of sending everyone home. But she hated to make them walk in the downpour. Perhaps it would stop by the time school was to let out.

She could feel the tension in the room, the children sneaking peeks at the windows just like she was. "All right, that's enough." She rose to her feet and headed for the piano that had been donated at Christmastime. "We can take an hour out and call this getting ready for the last day of school's concert."

The children cheered and gathered around her, the little ones in front and the taller in the back. They ran through some drills with Rebekka striking chords up a half each time. The "la, la, la, la, la, la, las" rang clear to the rafters. When she swung into "She'll Be Comin' 'Round the Mountain When She Comes," everyone laughed and joined in all the funny sounds.

Their "toot toot" stopped in midsound. Rebekka listened. Who was hollering? What was that roar? It sounded like three freight trains bearing down on them.

She leaped to her feet and ran to the windows facing south. In horror she saw gray water surging between them and the town. Waves rolled before chunks of ice, tearing at the banks and already climbing up to the schoolhouse steps. Out in the main channel of the Missouri, trees ripped past, tumbling in the flash flood that rose by inches each minute.

How would she get the children out?

"Everyone, over here. John, you get the jump ropes from the cloakroom. Everyone, grab your coats. And let us pray. "Father God, please help us. Amen."

She checked the windows on the north. A rise just beyond them was their only chance. Could the big ones help get the little ones there?

"Rebekka, Rebekka!" A male voice sounded from outside. "Help me open the door." Water that had begun seeping under the door, gushed in when it opened.

"Jude!" Rebekka had never been so glad to see anyone in her life.

"Okay, children, follow the instructions exactly!" Rebekka lined them up, little ones held by the bigger.

"Okay, kids, we have ropes out here and men to help you. Come on out, John, you stay there to help Miss Stenesrude." He grabbed Emily around the waist and handed her off to the next in line, the water lapping at his hips.

Rebekka kept her voice calm, even though she was screaming inside. "That's right. Next." One by one, the children were passed the long distance between the school and the rise.

The water covered the floor. Rebekka could feel a rocking motion, as if she were standing on the deck of a ship. The men stood in waist-deep water.

Rebekka didn't dare look at Jude for fear he'd see the panic in her eyes. "Thank You, God. Okay, John, you go now."

"You, too. Here, take my hand."

"Get out of here!" Jude yelled this time.

Rebekka felt the building shift again. Like a grand ship on her maiden voyage, the school slipped from its pilings and tipped forward.

"Jude!" Rebekka couldn't tell if she screamed or just thought it.

"Rebekka!" Jude pulled himself up into the cloakroom. "I have the rope. We have to swim for it." He grabbed her around the waist and flung them both into the swirling river.

Rebekka clung to his neck, trying to keep her head above the freezing water.

Jude's face had the gray cast of one who was cold beyond endurance.

She found the rope with one hand and kept her other around his rib cage.

"Hang on, my dearest," Jude said. "We're almost there." Three men waded out in the water and pulled the two ashore. Rebekka had never been so cold in her life. Her teeth chattered like castanets and she fell into the arms that held out blankets. "Jude, where's Jude?"

"Over there," someone answered. "We're trying to get him warmed. He's been in that freezing water longer than anyone."

"The children?" She could hardly force the words past her clacking teeth.

"Cold, but all right."

"Willowford?" She felt herself slipping into a gray place where she would sleep the pain in her feet away. She thought she heard a voice but could no longer answer. Peace and oblivion.

When she woke up, the lamp reminded her of sunrise. She opened her eyes and looked around. She lay in her room at the boarding-house. Had the flood been a dream?

"Here, drink this," Mrs. Sampson ordered as she held a cup to Rebekka's lips.

Rebekka sipped, then pushed herself to a sitting position. "I'm fine. Where's Jude?"

"Sleeping in his room. He has some frostbite on his feet, but he'll be okay."

"What about the flood?"

"Like all flash floods, as soon as they crest, they're gone. The Missouri is plenty high and still flooding, but the town is safe again." Mrs. Sampson turned at the sound of another voice. "There's that man again. He'da been in here hours ago if I'da let him."

"Jude?" Rebekka felt her cheeks widen. She could no longer keep the grin from busting forth. "How's the school?"

"Fine, or so they tell me." Jude stood in the door. "Just off its pinnings and downstream about two hundred yards. We built it good and sturdy. Should last a hundred years or so." He stared at the woman propped against the pillows. He'd come close to losing her and he'd never told her how much he loved her.

He gave the two widows a look that sent them laughing from the room. When he sat down on the bed, he took Rebekka's hand in his. "I asked God to save us."

"And He did."

"I can't ask you to marry me until I go home and make things right with my family."

"Marry you?"

"And I need to explain what happened in my life." He stroked the tender skin on the back of her hand.

"Jude."

"I know God forgives me now. I—"

"Jude." She placed her fingers gently against his lips. He raised his gaze from her hand to her face.

"I have one question." She studied the lines of his beloved face.

"What?"

"Do you love me?" She could feel the lump threatening to cut off her breathing.

"What kind of a question is that? Of course, I love you. What do you think I've been saying? But you have to know everything—"

"Then, yes." She reached for his strength, that formidable strength that had saved her and the children from the flood's waters. "I already know all the important things. What happened before has nothing to do with us." When he wrapped his arms around her, she snuggled into his chest. As she raised her face to look up at him, she caught a sheen in his eyes.

"That hymn you sang a while ago—'Throw out the lifeline...'" Rebekka nodded.

"Well, seems we needed one right bad and there it was." He kissed her eyes. "But I'm home now." He found her lips. "I almost lost you," he muttered into the side of her neck.

"I'm glad I found you," Rebekka answered.

The kiss they shared was all she'd dreamed of and feared never to experience. Together, they looked out the window to watch the sun sink into the horizon. Dusk settled into the room, bringing the peace of evening. But Rebekka knew. And now Jude knew, too. For every dusk there is a sunrise, and together they would face anything that came their way. They and the Savior who promised a bright new morning after the end of a long hard day.